Temporarily
In Love

DANICA FLYNN

Temporarily In Love

Copyright © 2022 Danica Flynn
This is a work of fiction. Names, characters, businesses, places, events, and incidents are either products of the author's imagination or used in a fictitious manner. Any resemblance to actual persons, living or dead, or actual events is purely coincidental.

All rights reserved.

Ebook ISBN: 978-1-957494-04-3
Print ISBN: 978-1-957494-05-0

Editors: Leah Francic & Kate Seger
Cover Design: Emily's World of Design
Cover Photography: DariYad & PantherMediaSeller/ Deposit Photos

For all my pumpkin spice hoes

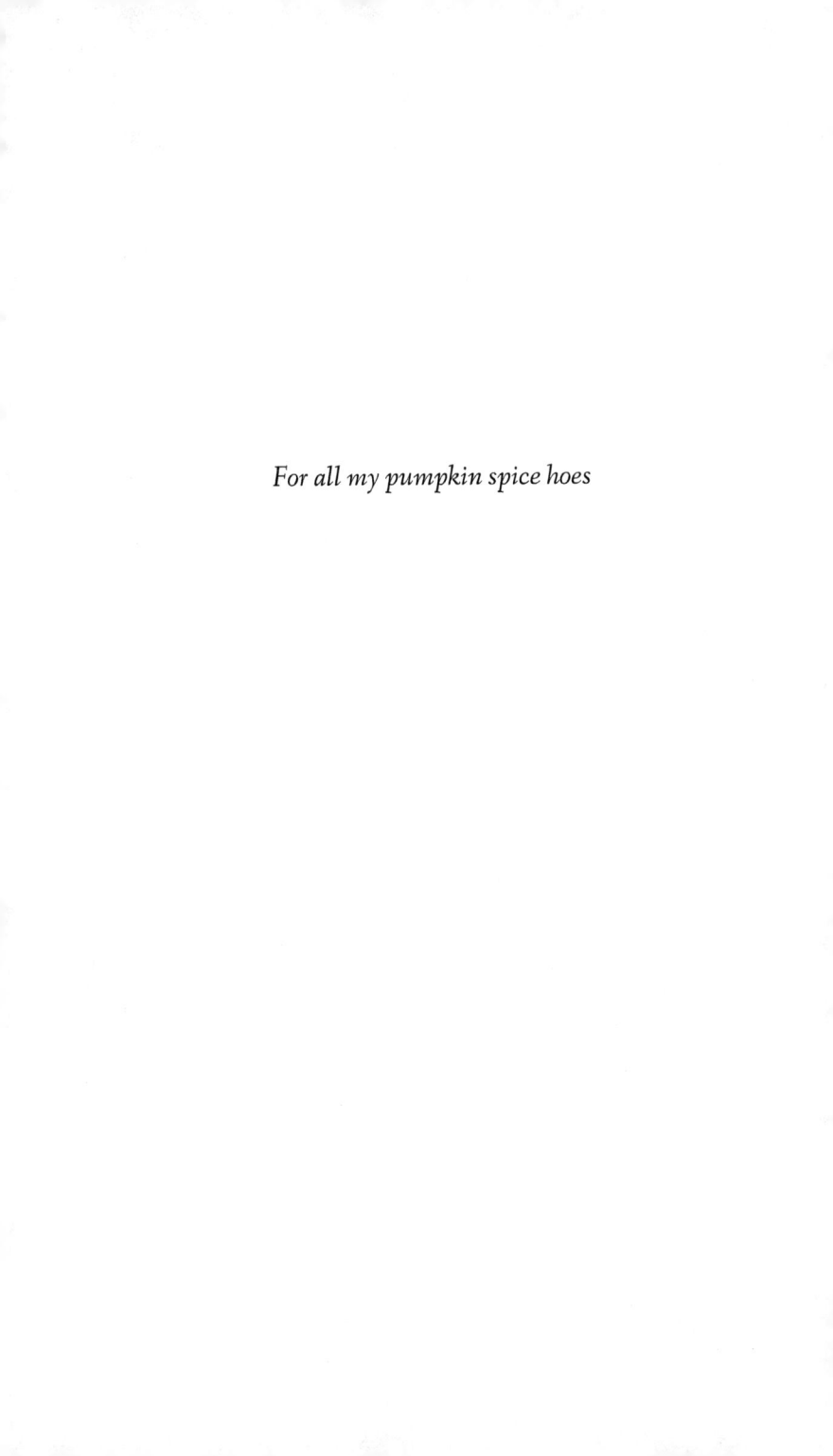

PLAYLIST

"Somebody That I Used To Know" By Gotye, Kimbra
"Hello" By Adele
"Baby I'm Crying" By Best Coast
"Irish Pub Son" By The High Kings
"Crush Culture" By Conan Gray
"San Francisco" By The Mowgli's
"Portion for Foxes" By Rilo Kiley
"Love Test" By The Growlers
"California Dreaming'" By Hazel English
"Under The Milky Way" By The Church
"Heat Waves" By Glass Animals
"Season of the Witch" By Lana Del Rey
"Black and Tans" By Scythian
"White Winter Hymnal" By Fleet Foxes
"The Killing Moon" By Echo & The Bunnymen
"I put a Spell on You" By Graham BLVD
"Thriller" By Michael Jackson
"House of the Rising Sun" By The Animals
"Idea of Her" By Cavetown

"Zombie" By The Cranberries
"Love me Like You Used To" By Lord Huron
"We fell in love in October" By Girl in Red

CHAPTER ONE

LILA

END OF SEPTEMBER

I always forgot what fall in Pennsylvania was like. The leaves turned color almost overnight, and the air got chilly enough that all you needed was a light jacket and a cup of hot cider. Maybe it was my imagination, but the town almost smelled of cinnamon and pumpkin, like it was teasing me for being gone for so long.

In California, you could find hipsters with big bushy beards wearing flannel and girls sipping on pumpkin spice lattes, but it wasn't the same as fall in Drakesville, Pennsylvania. Having lived on the other side of the country since college, my memory of what an East Coast fall looked like had slipped away.

When I walked up into the town square for the annual Arts Fest with my sister and her kids, fallen leaves crunched beneath my boots, reminding me of how much I loved this season. I marveled at how pretty the trees looked, painted in shades of red, yellow, and orange. If you've ever wanted to see how gorgeous autumn could be in my home state, come to Drakesville and see for yourself.

I pulled my plaid jacket around myself and shivered at the autumn air hitting me in the face. That prompted a laugh from my sister, Kelsey. "It's like sixty degrees. How are you cold?"

"This is cold for me!" I argued.

She laughed and shook her head as she held her toddler on her hip. "You've been in California too long. It's perfect weather for the Arts Fest."

My niece Callie babbled on my sister's hip as my other niece Cora clasped my hand and stomped on the leaves with me. My sister hadn't been happy about me encouraging that behavior. But how could you enjoy fall if you couldn't jump into the leaves?

I hadn't been back to town for my favorite season in years. I barely made it back for Thanksgiving or Christmas. Part of that was because I worked a demanding job as an intellectual property lawyer for a big tech company. The other part was that I actively avoided coming home at all costs. I'd do anything to avoid running into Declan MacGregor.

But when you caught your fiancé sleeping with his secretary and your mom called, saying your dad wanted to sell the family bar, you got your ass on a plane home to sort it all out.

Sullivan's Bar was a staple in our town, and I couldn't bear the thought of my dad selling it. So many things in town had changed since I left for Stanford. I didn't want the bar to be yet another one of those things.

Dad didn't want to talk about it when he picked me up from the airport last night. Instead, he kept asking me if I had set a date for my wedding. I hadn't told my family Chad and I had broken up yet. Or that I had quit my job because of it.

"Auntie Lila, can we get cookies from the bakery?" my niece asked, snapping me out of my thoughts.

"Ask your mommy," I said.

My sister frowned.

Cora was already hopped up on sugar because I was the fun aunt. That's what Kels got for berating me about being thirty-four with no babies of my own. I thought I'd have that soon, but a part of me was glad I never settled on a wedding date. Maybe deep down, I always knew it wasn't going to work out with Chad.

We hadn't been in a good place in a long time. When he proposed, I only said yes because I thought I was running out of time and options. I wanted a family, but my techie fiancé never made time for me, and we worked in the same damn building. Sure, he had more pressure on him as the CEO, but I worked the same soul-sucking hours. His cheating on me was only half the reason I sent in my resignation and headed home to Pennsylvania.

"Cora, no. You'll spoil your dinner," my sister warned and shot me a glare.

I ruffled Cora's red hair. "Sorry, kiddo. Hey, let's go over to the tattoo booth and get you a temporary tattoo."

Cora practically dragged me over to the booth. The tattoo shop, Tattooed Mamas, was female-owned, which I loved, and earlier, they were giving out temporary tattoos for the kids. It would distract Cora for a while.

"Hey, you!" Lizzie called out to me as we approached. We had been friends since high school, and while she still had the colorful lavender hair, now her body was painted with the ink of her profession. "Lila Sullivan, as I live and breathe."

I frowned. "As you live and breathe, really Liz?"

She shrugged. "I could have said, 'hey youse guys' instead, but I don't think you remember what it's like living in the Philly area anymore."

"Har har har. I still pronounce water 'wooder.' I didn't forget my roots," I said.

She laughed. "What was the first thing you did when you got to town?"

"Ate one of my dad's cheesesteaks!"

"What? You didn't stop at Pat's or Geno's on your way back from the airport?"

I scoffed. "What am I? A tourist?"

We laughed together. Pat's and Geno's were nowhere near the airport, but it was a joke we always made when I came to town. Only tourists who went to South Street went there.

Lizzie's eyes darted to my niece. "Hey, Cora. You want a tattoo?"

My little niece nodded. Lizzie smiled and brought Cora over to a chair behind the booth. Lizzie made a big production of putting the temporary tattoo on my niece's arm. She was good with kids like that, and I had a feeling she often did this with her own.

When it was done, Cora was all smiles and skipped over to me to show me the rainbow-colored butterfly tattoo on her bicep.

"Wow, look at that. Did that hurt?" I asked.

"Nope! I'm a big girl!" Cora said proudly.

I smiled at her and smoothed down her hair. "Yes, you are. Now, what do you say to Lizzie?"

"Thank you!" she told my friend.

Lizzie smiled at me. "Hey! You should come to the brewery later to get a beer with me after the fest."

I made a face.

I had no intention of ever stepping foot in the MacGregor Brothers Brewing Company. It might be a block away from my family's bar, and people raved about their beers, but I wasn't welcome there. And for good reason, too.

"You still haven't gone there?" Lizzie asked.

I shook my head.

"Lila, that was in high school. I'm sure Declan's over your breakup by now. It's been like fifteen years."

Sixteen, but who was counting? Oh right, me. Because I wasn't over the breakup with my high school sweetheart. I wasn't sure I ever could be. Even though I was the one to break up with him.

Every relationship since had failed because my heart only had room for Declan freaking MacGregor. It explained why when I found Chad with his secretary, I simply took off my engagement ring and placed it on his desk. I didn't even say anything to him. I sent him a formal email the next day informing him I was going out of town and wanted his stuff out of my house. If I had loved Chad, I wouldn't have done that. But I left my heart in Drakesville long ago, and it was the reason I avoided coming back. It hurt too much.

"Think about it!" Lizzie said.

"We better go." I waved at her while I walked with my niece to find my sister.

Unfortunately, Kelsey was exactly where I didn't want her to be. I found her standing in front of the brewery's booth, talking to a tall woman with pink hair and flower tattoos on her arm. The pink-haired lady looked excited and gestured wildly with her hands. I didn't recognize her, but she looked younger than me, so we probably never passed each other in school. Drakesville was a small town, but despite what Hallmark or the Gilmore Girls told you, you didn't know everyone and their business when you lived here.

Cora ran over to her mom, and my sister pretended to be wowed by the temporary tattoo on her daughter's arm. Kelsey was a good mom; at least she gave my parents some grandkids. My biological clock was ticking, and I didn't see that being an option for me anytime soon.

"Look who it is!" a big, booming voice said behind me.

I spun on my heel and came face-to-face with Nolan MacGregor.

He looked older than I remembered. He still had that big bushy beard, and coupled with his red plaid shirt, he looked like a burly lumberjack—like a husky Brawny Man. I scanned him, then narrowed my eyes when I noticed the baby strapped to his chest. The last I heard, Nolan and his wife divorced a couple of years ago. But maybe she had a change of heart, and that was a rumor.

"Hi, Nolan," I sighed.

"He's not around. He's doing spreadsheets," he said, fixing me with a warning glare. "And you better stay away."

"Excuse me?"

This wasn't the first time Nolan told me to piss off. The last time I saw him, I ran into him the next town over at the super grocery store, and he told me not to bother Declan while I was in town. Nolan was nothing if not fiercely protective of his little brother.

"You heard me, Lila. Stay away from my brother. He doesn't need you opening up that old wound again."

I couldn't ask Nolan what he meant because the baby on his chest started to cry. Nolan's scowl increased, but he took her out of the sling and rocked her. Watching the big bear of a man gently soothe his daughter was cute.

"Oh, there you are." A dark-haired petite woman with curves came up behind Nolan. She took the baby from his arms. "Aw, Peanut, be good for Daddy."

Okay, he definitely didn't have a baby with his ex-wife Kath. I didn't recognize the woman beside him, but she might not be a townie. She noticed me for the first time and gave me a sheepish look as she put the baby on her hip. "I'm sorry. Where are my manners? I'm Avery MacGregor. I don't think we've been introduced."

She held out her hand to me and we shook hands. "Lila Sullivan."

Her blue eyes lit up. "Oh! You're Kelsey's sister. We teach at the high school together." Avery saw me staring at her baby. "Do you want to hold her?"

"Oh. Can I?"

She nodded. "But fair warning, she likes to pull hair."

"And beards," Nolan muttered.

I smiled at that. It was good to know the more things changed in this town, the more they stayed the same, like Nolan MacGregor being a grump. Avery put the baby in my arms, who immediately tried to pull on my hair. I laughed and shook my long chestnut locks out of the way.

Avery chuckled. "Do you have kids? Seems like you have practice with this."

I shook my head as I held her baby, and my heart did a somersault at how she laid her little head on my chest and curled up into me.

"What's her name?" I asked.

"Norah," Nolan grunted.

"Oh," I sighed, and my heart panged at the memory of Norah MacGregor. "Oh, Nol, you're such a softie."

Avery beamed. "Yeah, he is."

Nolan scowled, but when Avery reached up on her tiptoes and gave him a kiss, a smile spread across his face. Kath never made him smile like that. I don't remember the last time I saw Nolan MacGregor smile. I could tell he loved his wife something fierce. And he had a baby. He looked so happy, and I never thought the grouch of a man would look like that.

"I can't believe you have a baby," I said.

Avery took Norah out of my arms as she started to fuss.

"I can't believe you showed your face in town again," Nolan shot back.

Avery arched an eyebrow at her husband. I wasn't about to tell her that her husband hated me because of what I did to his brother.

"Lila!" my sister called out to me, distracting me from the conversation. She walked over to me with a plastic cup of beer in her hand. "Here, have a beer," she said and handed it to me.

I wrinkled my nose. "No, thanks."

"It's a pumpkin beer. You love pumpkin," said a voice from behind me. A deep manly voice that I was hoping I'd never hear ever again.

Crap. This was why I never came home.

CHAPTER TWO

DECLAN

I should have been out on the floor checking that my servers didn't need help. Or in the loft, making sure the art show was going off without a hitch. Or over in the town square, ensuring our booth for the Arts Fest had everything it needed.

What was I doing instead? Burying myself in spreadsheets. Because that's what I did. I ran the numbers, did logistics, and managed the front end while my older brother Nolan brewed the beers. Thank god Gemma finally took the marketing director job over the summer, or I would have been doing that too. My big brother, god love him, was good at brewing beer, but he wasn't a business guy.

A knock on my office door brought me out of my thoughts. I realized I had been staring at the numbers on my spreadsheet and not getting any work done. One of our bartenders, Felix, stood in the doorway, rubbing his tattooed hand across his beard nervously.

"Yo, boss man," he said.

"What's up?" I asked and took my glasses off. I rubbed the bridge of my nose in frustration. I usually wore my contacts, but spreadsheets hurt my eyes, so those were always glasses days.

Felix raked his hand through his shaggy black hair. "Wyatt had to call out sick, so we're understaffed at the booth. I can't go because it's only me and Asher behind the bar here."

This expense report wasn't getting done until later. I saved my document and shut down my computer. "I'll handle it."

"You sure, man?" Felix asked.

I waved him off. "I got it."

"Tell my girl she looks hot!"

I shook my head at him. "Ew, I'm not telling Gemma that!"

He smirked at me and walked off. I thought Felix and Gemma were great together, but since they were still so new, they were kind of annoying. Like my brother and his wife. I knew they weren't trying to shove their happiness in my face, but sometimes it was too much to deal with.

I smoothed my shirt down as I stood up from my desk. I grabbed my wallet and keys, and walked out of the office, shutting the door behind me. It was a short walk from the brewery to the town square where the Arts Fest was being held.

I didn't mind picking up the slack for my employees when I needed to. That was what the boss was supposed to do. Nolan and I both did that because we wanted our brewery to succeed. Also, because we were both workaholics. That probably stemmed from our parents dying when I was twelve and Nolan was eighteen. Growing up, I watched my older brother struggle to keep a roof over our heads. He worked his fingers to the bone until I went to Penn State on a scholarship.

Booths from all the local businesses lined the town square as I walked up and found ours. I saw Gemma talking to Kelsey Sullivan, who had one kid on her hip and the other hugging onto her leg. Kelsey always reminded me of Lila, the girl who broke my heart when I was eighteen. She went to college in California and never came back, leaving me shattered. It was the reason I stayed away from Sullivan's Bar in town. There were too many memories there.

I spied Nolan and Avery talking to a brunette woman, who I couldn't place because she had her back to me. All I could see was that she had a fantastic ass. The kind I'd love to spank while I had her pressed face-down on my bed.

Damn, I needed to get laid.

Kelsey called her over, and when I heard the name on her lips, I wanted to back away slowly. Lila rarely showed her face in town since she left. She visited for holidays, but we did a good job avoiding each other.

Kelsey handed Lila a beer, but Lila shook her head. "No, thanks," she said.

"It's a pumpkin beer. You love pumpkin," I blurted out.

Lila spun on her heel and stared at me, her mouth ajar.

I should have walked away when I noticed her. I should have told Felix to go to the booth while I handled being behind the bar. I didn't want to be staring into the golden-flecked eyes of the woman I was still deeply in love with.

"Hey, Declan," she said, looking as uncomfortable as I felt.

My eyes roamed down her body. She looked so seasonal in her purple sweater and black skirt with a red plaid jacket. Despite being the end of September, it wasn't that cold yet, but she was dressed like someone who hadn't lived in Pennsylvania in a long time. Or at least someone who didn't bother to check the weather. Her hair looked about the same. Her flowing dark locks looked like the kind you wanted to bury your face in or grab into a fist while you fucked her into submission.

Don't think about fucking your ex. Do not do it.

"Hey, Lila," I said flatly.

"Here, take the beer," Kelsey urged, shoving the plastic cup into her sister's face.

Lila rolled her eyes, but took the drink from her sister. She sipped on it slowly, and her eyes lit up. She turned back to my brother. "Oh my god, Nolan, this is amazing."

Avery beamed. "Isn't it good?"

"It's like a pumpkin spice latte in beer form!" Lila cheered and took another sip.

I took that as my leave to slip past her and get behind the booth. Annie was managing the booth alone, and she gave me a look of relief. "Oh, thank god, it's been nuts today."

I checked the lines on the keg we had in the booth and made sure we were okay. "That's good for business."

She beamed at me and tossed her blonde hair over her shoulder. "Definitely."

I pretended to ignore that flirtatious gesture. Annie made it known she was interested, but I didn't date employees. I hooked up with one of the servers a couple of years ago, and it ended badly when she realized I was only looking for a few nights.

Gemma was supposed to talk to Annie about that, but I wasn't sure if it had helped. Or if Annie had listened.

Lila laughed with Avery as they gushed over The Drake Pumpkin Ale. Nolan made that pumpkin beer last year for Avery and knocked her up almost immediately. I hadn't been a fan of doing that beer, but Nolan wanted to branch out and try something different. The numbers didn't lie; it had been a hit. Then when he made the hefeweizen beer this past summer, the numbers hadn't lied either. Maybe it was okay to do stuff other than typical IPAs and pale ales.

"Who's that?" Annie asked.

"Who?"

"The pretty brunette Avery's talking to."

"Nobody," I muttered.

Annie eyed me curiously, but couldn't ask the question she was dying to ask because we had another couple of customers come up to the booth. Lila and her sister moved on, thank god. My brother stood off to the side of the booth, watching me like a hawk.

"You good?" he mouthed.

I nodded, and he walked off with Avery to check out the rest of the festival. Probably to feed her dumplings again like he did last year. They were so gross and in love, but I was glad my big brother finally found his one true love after his train wreck of a first marriage.

Annie took the customer's order while I got them their beers. She took their money and put it in the cash box. My eye twitched when she put the money in the wrong way. I opened up the cashbox and redid it, so everything was facing the right way.

"Declan, you're so anal," she said with a laugh.

Anal, maybe, but I liked things neat and orderly. Things had to be a certain way, or I wasn't in control, and I had to be in control.

"Thanks for coming to help," she said and squeezed my arm.

"It's my job," I stated flatly, not looking at her.

Instead, I stared out into the crowd, searching for Lila. Because of course I was.

Like me, she was older now, but she still made my heart skip a beat when I saw her. I didn't know why she was in town. She worked for some big-time tech company out in Silicon Valley, so it didn't make sense that she was back in Pennsylvania. It wasn't even a holiday.

I spent the next couple of hours manning the booth with Annie until the festival was over. Nolan and Gemma came back to help break everything down and take it back to the brewery. Gemma was on a roll with getting our name out there since she took over marketing. I hadn't even questioned her when she asked me to sign the permit applications for the Harvest Fest next weekend. The annual fall carnival in the fairgrounds a couple towns over brought in a huge crowd, so having a booth there made sense.

I should have gone home to get some sleep, but there was still so much I needed to get done. When we got everything back to the brewery, I logged onto my computer and finished up my expense report. I still needed to do payroll, and that couldn't wait. I needed to make sure everyone got paid on time.

"Dude, go home," my brother said to me.

I looked up and saw him standing in the doorway of the office. "I got shit to do. Go home and be with Avery and Norah."

"Nah, I'm finishing the last batch of the new Christmas beer."

"Yeah, you got a name yet?"

He shrugged. "It's for Avery. So Avery's Ale?"

"Booooo!" I yelled at him.

That was why I had wanted Gemma to be the

marketing director. She was way better at naming shit. Nol sucked at catchy names.

My brother scowled at me, but that was nothing new. My big brother was the grumpiest person I knew. "Man, don't be a dick."

"Ask Gemma for a suggestion. That's her job. Then she'll have Felix work on the design for the labels."

The scowl didn't leave his face.

"What? I gotta finish payroll. What do you want?"

"Are you okay?"

I furrowed my brow at him. "Yeah?"

Nolan rubbed a hand through his big, bushy beard. I never understood how he dealt with having that thing; beards were too itchy for me. I preferred being clean-cut.

"Lila Sullivan's back in town."

"So what?"

He glared at me. "I know you still have feelings for her. So don't let her put her spell on you again."

"Don't you have a family to bother?" I asked, hoping he'd leave me alone.

I didn't want to talk about Lila or how I was still in love with her. After all these years, even after dating so many other women, I was still enamored with a girl who broke up with me because she wanted to chase her dreams.

"Shame about the bar, though," Nolan mused.

I cocked an eyebrow at him. "What about it?"

"You didn't hear?"

I shook my head. "Hear what?"

"Sean's selling the bar."

I reared back at that. Sean Sullivan was selling the family bar? That didn't make sense to me. Sullivan's was a staple in our town and had been in the family for generations. When our parents died, and Nolan needed a quick way to make sure we still had food on the table, Sean gave him a job without question. Because the Sullivans had been our parents' closest friends.

If it wasn't for Nolan working there, he never would have started tending bar. Never would have chatted up the local brewers that did business with the bar. We never would have started home brewing until I had a solid business plan and secured a loan to start our own operation. Sullivan's was the first bar that took our beers.

"What?" I asked in disbelief.

Nolan nodded. "I think that's why Lila's in town."

"Huh."

He checked his phone and smiled, which meant Avery had sent him a text. He only smiled when it came to her and their baby. Before Nolan got Avery pregnant and had a shotgun wedding here at the brewery, he was the grouchiest asshole I'd ever met. I loved Avery for making him less of a grumpasaurus.

"Don't stay too late. You need to take a break," he said and gave me a stern look.

"You're worse than me, so don't even try it," I argued.

He sighed. "Yeah, but Avery made me see that you need a good work-life balance. With her and the baby, I have something to go home to. As much as I love the brewery, you can't be at your best when you're all work and nothing else."

"Yeah, yeah, yeah. I have to finish payroll at least."

"Leave before close," he said and walked out.

But I didn't leave before close. Felix and Asher had to come into the office to tell me they were locking up. I was able to get payroll done, but there was still so much to do. Tomorrow was another day, and I could worry about that then.

I walked out of the brewery and headed for my apartment above the tattoo shop. It wasn't very big, but a few years ago, I wanted my own space away from Nolan. I was grateful I had already moved out when Avery got pregnant and moved in with my brother. Watching them start their family together would've been annoying. Unlike Nolan, I didn't have anyone waiting for me at home. That was why I worked myself to death for the brewery. It was the only thing that mattered in my life.

CHAPTER THREE

LILA

*D*amn, this was a good beer, and I was mad about it. I sipped the pumpkin beer from the MacGregor Brothers Brewing Company as I sat on a barstool in my parents' bar. I hadn't caught the name yesterday, but when Dad asked me what I thought of The Drake Pumpkin Ale, I laughed.

I pushed my plate of half-eaten cheesesteak away and drank the rest of my beer. Dad went to get me a box since he knew I never finished meals in one sitting.

I looked around the bar and tried to suss out why Dad wanted to sell it. When you thought of a typical Irish bar, you probably thought of a pub with a dark wood interior, dim lights, and signs for Guinness or the Ireland flag. Whatever you pictured, that was exactly what Sullivan's Bar looked like. It was old-timey, yet perfect, and the idea of my dad selling it crushed me.

Dad came back with the to-go container and boxed up the rest of the cheesesteak for me. We might be an Irish bar, but we were also a bar outside of Philadelphia, so we had to have cheesesteaks on the menu. When I moved to California, I once saw something called 'A Philly' on a menu, and I laughed my butt off because no one called them that here. And then it was the worst thing I ever ate. There was mayo on it. MAYO! It was a travesty.

"Dad, do you really have to sell?" I asked.

He grimaced. "Afraid so, honey."

He ran a frustrated hand across his scruffy jaw. My dad's age was starting to show. He was in his mid-sixties and looked tired from working his fingers to the bone in the bar all his life. His red hair had gone shock white when I was a teenager, but his face looked more tired now.

"Why?" I asked again.

"The business isn't doing so well."

I started calculating some things in my head. I had a lot of money. I lived in a massive house in Silicon Valley and worked eighty-plus hours a week. I could afford to help the bar and save it.

"How long are you in town for? When do you have to go back to work?" he asked, trying to change the subject.

Yeah, about that.

I still hadn't told my parents that Chad and I had broken up or that I had quit my job. I'd have no problem finding another job, but I wasn't sure I wanted to work in tech anymore. Or even as a lawyer. I was exhausted and unhappy, and coming home might have been just what I needed.

"I don't have to go back," I said.

He eyed my left hand for the third time since I came over to the bar for lunch. "Honey, what's going on?"

I sighed. "Chad cheated on me."

"Bastard! Never liked him."

"Me neither, honestly," I said. "I can't work for his company anymore, so I quit and cashed in on all the vacation time I never took."

Dad narrowed his eyes. "That's not the real reason you came home, though, huh? You actively avoid it."

"Dad, you know how it is in this town. Everyone hates me for what I did to Declan MacGregor."

Dad laughed. "I don't think even the MacGregor Brothers hate you. Declan was in here last summer, and he looked more sad than angry."

"Dad! That's worse! I don't want to know that he's been pining after me all this time."

Dad rolled his eyes. "He's definitely not been pining, honey. He's a grown-ass man, and you're a grown-ass woman. You broke up fifteen years ago."

Sixteen years ago, but I wasn't going to correct him.

He prodded my arm. "Why are you home now? I know you're not brokenhearted over that asshat."

I had to laugh at that. My dad said what he was thinking at all times. That's what I loved about him. It was so refreshing to be back on the East Coast, where people didn't talk in circles like in the tech world.

"I don't want you to sell the bar."

"Honey, I have to."

"Okay, what if I helped you with the finances? We could hire a marketing or PR firm. If you had the capital—"

"I'm not taking your money!"

"Dad! Sullivan's been in the family for generations. I want it to stay that way. I love this bar. I'm willing to be a silent partner if you want. I want my kids to know their history. And my grandkids. I don't want to see the family's legacy disappear."

He squinted at me. "You and your sister are annoying, you know that?"

"You raised us," I teased.

Mom came out of the kitchen and smiled when she saw me sitting at the bar. We had strategically set this up so I could talk to Dad alone. Mom was looking her age as well. Her dark brown hair had silver streaks, and she looked tired. I hated that my parents were still working at this point in their lives.

"Hey, sweetheart. Are you ready to go?" she asked.

"Dad, can you leave my food in the fridge? I'll be back."

Dad gave us a suspicious look. "Where are you two off to?"

Mom waved him away. "I told you! Gemma Jensen agreed to give me some marketing advice. We're heading over to the brewery. We'll be back in a few."

Wait, oh no. Mom never said we were meeting this Gemma lady at the brewery. Why were we meeting her at the brewery? I hadn't agreed to that.

"Wait. Why can't she meet us here?" I asked.

Mom shook her head. "Because I like the food there!"

"Rude!" my dad teased.

"Love you, hon, but I'm sick of our food!" my mom called back and blew him a kiss.

When I was a kid, my parents being in love seemed gross, but now I thought it was sweet that they still loved each other after all these years. I wished I could have that.

Mom urged me along, and I reluctantly hopped off the barstool and followed her outside. The brewery was only a block down the street, so it wasn't a far walk. I hadn't stepped foot in the brewery, ever, so I felt like my mom did this on purpose.

She made comments every year about how Declan was

such a nice young man, and some woman would snap him up soon. Her way of telling me we should get back together. But I broke his heart when I went away to Stanford. Especially since I never told him I was applying.

I was all set to go to Penn State with him, but my guidance counselor encouraged me to apply to my dream school. I never thought I'd get accepted. It had been a great opportunity that I couldn't turn down. But then I waited until the last possible second, never telling Declan I wasn't going with him. I took the coward's way out, breaking up with him and leaving the very next day. I didn't call, and I barely came home. If I had, I wouldn't have finished my degree. I would have stayed in this tiny little town and never made a career for myself. Even if I wasn't particularly happy with that career anymore.

"So you broke it off with Chad?" Mom asked as we walked down the street together.

"You heard me tell Dad?"

She nodded. "Also, you're not wearing your ring, and you moved your Claddagh ring back to your right hand."

Of course she noticed that.

"Why did you quit too?"

"I couldn't work for his company anymore."

She frowned as we waited at the crosswalk for the little green man on the signal to light up. My Mom turned her hazel eyes on me. "Sweetheart, tell the truth."

I sighed. "I'm not sure I want to work in tech anymore. Everyone's full of shit and thinks they're god's gift to the world. The money's good, like really good, but I'm unhappy."

"Maybe you could be a lawyer close to home," Mom suggested.

I didn't argue with her because she sped off across the

street, and I followed behind her. Yeah, I saw that one coming. Mom hated that I was so far away from the rest of the family. Even our extended family still lived in or around the Philly area. I was the weird cousin who went off far away for college.

We walked past the tattoo shop where my friend Lizzie worked, and then we were at the door of the brewery. Kelsey said there was a brewery here before the MacGregors, but the place had been an old Rolls Royce showroom when we were kids. Mom held open the heavy door, and we walked inside together.

The Rolls Royce thing made sense once I stepped inside. The interior was open with high ceilings, and I spied an upstairs area that looked like a loft. The bar was towards the back of the room, with a bunch of tables and chairs set up in the front. On the right, glass windows showed the tanks where Nolan and an older Black man were having an intense conversation. Artwork that matched the style of the beer labels hung on the walls, and there was a big sign behind the bar with the brewery's logo above it.

The part of my heart that still loved Declan swelled with pride at what he and his brother had created. I tried to tamp that feeling down. I had no right to be proud of him. Not after what I did.

"I love what they did with the place," Mom said.

It was a cool space, but I didn't have time to say anything because the pink-haired woman my sister had been talking to at the Arts Fest came over to us.

My mom smiled at her. "Hey, Gemma. Thanks for meeting with us."

Gemma gestured to a table in front of us and we took our seats. One of the bartenders came over to take our order. He had dark hair and an eyebrow piercing. Like Gemma, he had a bunch of tattoos. Only both of his arms were covered, whereas Gemma only had one arm fully tattooed. He looked at Gemma like he wanted to make a meal out of her.

I only ordered water since I had already eaten, and I refused to give the MacGregors the satisfaction that I liked their beer.

"What do you want, sweet thing?" the bartender asked Gemma.

She beamed at him like a ray of freaking sunshine. "You always know what I want."

He smirked at her. "Well, I can't give that to you right now."

She waved him away. "Get me the goat cheese salad. You know what I like. And behave!"

He gave her a wink before he walked away. She gave us an apologetic look. "Sorry, that's my man. He can be such a horndog."

Mom laughed. "Glad you two are back together and you're not getting drunk in my bar asking for a job."

A guilty look crossed Gemma's face. I side-eyed my mom. I wanted to know what she was talking about. Okay, maybe this town made everyone a little gossipy. I shouldn't care what Mom was talking about, but I did. I kind of wanted to know the story about Gemma and the hot bartender.

Gemma gave me a smile and held out her hand. "Sorry, I didn't even introduce myself. I'm Gemma Jensen."

I shook her hand firmly. "Lila Sullivan."

"I've heard," she said in a way that made me wonder if she had heard from my family or Declan.

"Gemma, thanks for talking to us today," my mom swiftly changed the subject. "What sort of ideas do you have for us?"

Gemma smiled and opened up a notebook I hadn't noticed was in her hands. "Okay, so a couple of things. The first thing that came to mind was doing some collabs. I talked to Nolan about making an Irish Red beer and having it only at the brewery and your bar. I have an idea for a name, but Declan thought it was offensive."

"Why?" I asked.

"I was thinking of Old Man Sullivan," Gemma said.

My mom broke out into a big belly laugh. "Sean will love that!"

Gemma's smile brightened. "We'll probably want to do a draft for that, but we could do a limited bottle release. Oh, also, we have a booth at the Harvest Fest this weekend, so we could split it to get your name out." She looked down at her notebook. "So, I think you should play up the Irish thing."

"How so?" I asked.

"So your menu's great for pub food. It's got awesome American-style food. You got your flatbreads, appetizers, burgers, and some bigger entrees. But for an Irish bar, you don't have any traditional food."

"We have fish and chips," I said.

Gemma nodded. "Right, but maybe add something like a 'traditional Irish food' section. You could do an Irish stew, shepherd's pie, and maybe some boxtys."

"Bangers and mash too," Mom suggested.

"Maybe pasties too. We could do beef or potato ones for vegetarians," I suggested.

Gemma's smile got bigger. "Yes, exactly! I think if you lean into that more, it could help be a reason people want to come to the bar. Also, who did your website? It could use a revamp. And your social media's been absent."

I cringed. "Okay, yes, I agree with you."

"We can't afford it," my mom argued.

I held up my hand. "Mom, I'll pay for the redesign. Gemma, I know you can't do this job. But do you have any recommendations for someone who might be able to help, at least with our social media?"

"If money's a problem, see if someone on staff's social media savvy. That's what happened with me."

I nodded. "Okay, this is great info. Thank you so much for taking this time with us today."

"Oh, Declan told me I had to, but I don't mind."

I felt frozen in place at her words.

Declan told me I had to.

What the heck? What did that even mean?

Before I could ask, I saw something move out of the corner of my eye. I looked up and saw the man in question walking toward us with a baby in his arms. Did Declan have a kid?

My ovaries melted at the sight of him holding the baby to his chest as he tried to get her to stop fussing. There was a time I imagined a future with Declan where we'd have the big wedding and settle down with kids of our own. Maybe it was because my body wanted a baby, but seeing him holding one did something primal to me.

Gemma's eyes lit up when she saw Declan and the baby. "Aw, gimme her!"

Declan handed over the baby. "She's being cranky right now."

"Just like her dad!" Gemma said as she bounced the baby in her arms. "Huh, Peanut? You know you missed Auntie Gemma."

I realized the baby was Nolan's baby, not Declan's. A part of me breathed a sigh of relief. But that was unfair. I broke up with Declan years ago.

"Hey, Mrs. Sullivan. Did Gemma help you out?" Declan asked my mom, pointedly ignoring me.

"Yes, thanks so much. You looked good with that baby in your arms. When are you gonna have one of your own?" Mom asked.

"Mom," I hissed.

Declan laughed. "Not anytime soon."

Why did I perk up at that? I shouldn't care. But I did. I cared so much.

I met Declan's eyes, but it was like he looked through me. He had a pair of plastic frames on his face and was freshly clean-shaven, just the way I liked. He wore a neatly pressed polo shirt and jeans that looked brand new. He was so neat and put together. My type of man had clearly never changed.

"Hey, Lila," he said to me with an edge of strained politeness.

"Hi, Declan. Long time no see."

His jaw ticked in annoyance. "Yeah, well, that was your choice." He turned to Gemma. "Can you watch her for a bit? Nolan wasn't supposed to come in until later, but they had an issue with one of the tanks, and he needed to sort it out. I got shit to do."

Gemma nodded. "Of course. She's my niece too."

He spun on his heel and walked off into the back.

I cringed.

"Oh, woof. He's usually not like that," Gemma said.

I looked down at my lap. "It's okay. I deserve it."

Mom gave my arm a little squeeze. "Come on girlie, let's go talk to your dad about all this. Thanks so much, Gemma."

"No problem," Gemma said as we walked off.

I wasn't thinking about the suggestions Gemma gave us.

Instead, my mind was on the venom in Declan's voice. He had every right to hate me after I broke up with him. It had been the right decision, but I wished I hadn't hurt him so badly. Instead of taking the coward's way out, I should have been honest with him. Losing my best friend had been the hardest thing I ever went through. I couldn't imagine what it had been like for him, so I deserved every ounce of his hatred.

I walked out of the brewery with my mom and mulled it all over. Before we went back to the bar, she put a hand on the door to stop me. "Lila, tell me the truth."

"About what?"

She pinned me with that 'mom look.' The kind she gave you when she knew you were lying. "Do you still have feelings for Declan?"

I grimaced.

"Lila Catherine!"

"Yes," I muttered.

"Then maybe you should do something about it now that you're home."

That didn't even make sense. I was only home to make sure the bar would be okay. I wasn't going to stay in Drakesville.

CHAPTER FOUR

DECLAN

Why was Lila Sullivan in my freaking brewery? And why did seeing her make me act like a petulant child? That wasn't like me. I knew I should go out and apologize. She broke up with me in high school; I should be over it. But I wasn't.

Before I could go back out to the floor with my tail between my legs, Gemma burst into the office.

She put her hands on her hips and gave me an annoyed look.

"What?" I growled and took my glasses off to rub the bridge of my nose.

"You're a fucking asshole, is what."

I groaned and put my glasses back on. "Gemma, not now."

"Why don't you tell her you still love her? You were practically eye-fucking!" she exclaimed.

I sighed. Of course, Gemma wouldn't leave it alone.

When she and Felix were broken up, Kelly Sullivan

called me because Gemma was way too drunk at the bar. I hadn't exactly wanted to go there, but Gemma was making a scene. I took her to my apartment to sleep it off, and she prodded me about why I didn't like to go to Sullivan's. I let it slip that I still had feelings for my high school girlfriend. Now I regretted it because Gemma was getting that wild look in her eye like she was up to something.

"Gemma," I warned.

"Dude! Everyone can tell you still have feelings for each other. You didn't see how she looked at you when she saw you with Norah."

I put my glasses on and arched an eyebrow at her. "How did she look at me?"

"Like her ovaries melted," Gemma said with a sly grin.

I shook my head. "That's definitely not true. I should apologize, though, right?"

She shook her head and took her seat at the desk on the other side of the room. "You missed your chance. They already left."

"Thanks for helping them," I muttered and turned back to my computer.

"Mmmhmm," Gemma said as she buried herself in her work.

Gemma and I worked in silence for a little while. I was glad she finally agreed to take the marketing director job because she was really good at it. But since it was Gemma, she had to be a pain in the ass and refuse to take it to the point I forced her to go on vacation to think about it. Then she quit like a numbskull. I was so glad when she got back together with Felix and came back. I couldn't do a lot of stuff without her.

"Why did you ask me to help them if you hate Lila so much?" she asked.

I sighed. "I don't hate her."

"Sounded like it earlier."

"Seeing her opened up old shit I don't want to talk about. Okay, Gem?"

"Geez, you're wound so tight. You probably need to get laid to release that tension."

She was probably right, but I didn't want anyone in my bed right now.

I didn't bother to answer her. Instead, I finished working on the new HR training I wanted all the employees to complete. And the survey about the work environment.

I wanted to be a good boss. I was the sweet to Nolan's sour, but I wanted the brewery to be a place where people wanted to work. Just because we didn't want to 'be corporate' didn't mean we should be lax with certain things.

"I told Annie you had a girlfriend," Gemma said.

"Why?"

"So she'd lay off."

"Thanks, Gem."

"She thirsty!"

I laughed. "Christ, Gem."

She laughed with me. "What? I told her it was inappropriate to date her boss, and it was like in one ear and out the other. So maybe get a girlfriend soon?"

"Or maybe I have one, and she lives in Canada," I joked.

Gemma laughed and went back to work. I worked at my desk for a while before going out on the floor. Nolan and I were hands-on owners. We wanted to make sure our staff was happy, and if we were short-staffed, we pitched in.

I should be content with working regular hours in the back office, but I did more. While my brother brewed the beer, I was doing everything a manager should do. Like busing tables because we had an odd rush in the middle of the afternoon.

"Did you take a break today?" Nolan asked, and I jumped because his voice had startled me. He had Norah strapped to his chest, and she was fast asleep.

"Not yet," I said.

"Have a late lunch with me."

I arched an eyebrow at him. Nolan never took breaks, either. I usually had to be the voice of reason and pull him out to make sure he ate. I was pretty sure I was such a workaholic because he raised me that way.

"Allen said I was being crankier than the baby," he said at my unasked question.

I glared at him. "Did you have her in the tank room with you?"

"Fuck no! Felix watched her while he was on his lunch break."

"Okay, good."

"Did you think I'd take my fucking baby near the hops?" he snarled.

"I don't know!"

"Peanut was hanging with Uncle Fe today."

Since Felix was with Gemma, he was basically family now too, and had been relegated to Uncle Felix. He didn't mind because he was good with kids, even though he and Gemma didn't want any of their own.

I went over to the register behind the bar and punched in our orders. Nolan sat at one of the booths next to the bar and put Norah into her carrier. He fussed with her as he woke her up, and a smile turned up on my lips at watching my brother with his daughter. I was happy he got what he always wanted with Avery. She brought him out of his shell, and I loved that about her.

I sat across from Nolan and gave Felix a nod in thanks when he brought us over waters and beers.

Nolan rocked Norah's carrier to get her to fall back to sleep. "I saw Lila Sullivan here earlier."

I mumbled to myself.

"What was that about?"

"I told Gemma to give them marketing advice."

"Oh right. She told me about the Irish Red idea."

Felix came over with our food, and we chowed down in silence for a few minutes. I sipped on my glass of water and avoided my brother's look, but I could tell what he was about to say.

Nolan chewed on a fry. "I told Lila to stay away from you."

"You what?" I asked, sending him a death glare from across the table. Why the fuck would he do that?

He scowled. "Every time Lila comes to town, you spiral. You go back to being that eighteen-year-old kid standing in the driveway with his heart in his hands."

Half the time, I didn't even see Lila when she visited, but I heard about it because people in this town liked to ask if I'd seen her. Maybe Nolan was right, because I felt like my head was somewhere else, and I've only said a few sentences to her since she got back.

"I'm a grown-ass man, Nolan," I hissed at him. "You don't have to do that shit."

He shrugged and drank his beer. "Yeah, but man, you need to get over her."

"I know," I muttered sadly and ate one of my fries. "Imagine if Avery left you."

He scowled at me. "Why the fuck would you say that? Avery and I are solid. I'm not taking this ring off my finger, and she's not taking hers off."

I held up a hand to calm him down. He was getting heated about the mere suggestion of him and his wife breaking up. "Imagine if she left, and you had to figure out how to move on, but no one else ever measured up to her."

He stroked his beard in thought and had a worried look on his face. "Okay, I get it. But you dated in freaking high school."

"Lila was my best friend since the third grade. She was my everything."

"And what's she now?"

I sighed. "Nothing."

"So get over her already! It's not like she's moving back to Drakesville."

I nodded. He was right. I knew he was right, but my brain was thinking of all the what-ifs—of why, exactly, Lila was in town and how long she was going to stay.

"Did Gemma say if they wanted to make the beer?" Nolan asked.

I shrugged.

Nolan nodded. "All right, I'll ask her. It would take a while to make anyway. Are we good for the Harvest Fest this weekend?"

I nodded. "Yeah. Gemma worked her magic. I just had to sign off on some permits."

Nolan looked at his calendar on his phone. "Okay...we have a schedule for that, right? I can be there all day—"

"No! You spend your weekend with your family. I got this. Plus, as I told you before, we have a staff that's supposed to do this shit for us. Gemma wants to be there since this is her baby. If we're gonna split the table with the Sullivans, we might not need everyone."

Nolan nodded. "Okay, but I think Avery wanted to go

anyway, so we'll stop by with the baby. Who knows how long, though."

Norah made herself known with a loud cry and Nolan picked her up. I laughed when she immediately grabbed his beard. The little stinker was like that, but she was so cute, none of us could be mad at her. I was thankful I didn't have a beard, so she couldn't do that to me.

I rubbed my clean-shaven jaw and pointed at my brother's ridiculous mountain man beard. "You gotta shave that shit."

He made an annoyed face. "Nope, then Avery *would* divorce me."

I gave him a confused look.

"My wife loves her beard rides. I'm not getting rid of this, ever."

I pretended to puke. "Gross!"

Nolan shrugged and bounced his daughter in his arms. "That's how Mommy and Daddy created this little one, huh, Peanut? Did Daddy make Mommy forgetful, and we made you, you little stinker?"

I rolled my eyes at his baby talk to her, but it was cute. I was secretly jealous that I was still single and childless. I wanted to be a father, and there wasn't a time limit for guys, but I didn't want to be ancient when my kid graduated college. I wasn't sure that was ever in the cards for me. Especially since I was still hung up on the girl I dated in high school.

Who knows? My brother didn't become a father until he was forty. I still had a good six years to catch up to him. Maybe I'd meet my soulmate soon and get everything I ever wanted. The cynical part of me laughed bitterly at the thought.

CHAPTER FIVE

LILA

It took some convincing, but Dad agreed to all the changes Gemma suggested. He laughed his head off at the beer name, which was good. There was still a lot to do, so I started researching web designers and marketing firms.

My brother-in-law found me in the back office, scowling at my laptop. Brian was a big man. He was about six-foot-three and came from a family of loud-mouth Irish boys. He and Kelsey had been high school sweethearts, and he doted on my sister.

"Hey, Lila," he said.

"Hey! You coming on shift?" I asked.

Brian had been working at the bar since he was eighteen, waiting tables until Dad slowly grew to trust him. Now he was the manager and did a lot of the stuff my dad was 'too old to want to deal with anymore.' Dad's words, not mine.

"Did you talk to Gemma?" he asked.

I nodded. "We need to redo the website and get someone to do our social media. We have zero presence."

He nodded. "Right. I've asked one of the more tech-savvy servers to help with social. But I think we need the webmaster to relinquish control."

I groaned. "He still has control?"

Brian laughed. "Yeah, girl! But he makes updates anytime Pops asks. What did Pops say about all of Gemma's suggestions?"

"He's good with them. Level with me. How bad is it?"

Brian grimaced. "It's bad, kiddo."

I frowned. "I don't want us to lose the bar. I love the bar."

"Me too. Talk to Declan about the website."

I sighed. "Can you do it?"

He raised an eyebrow. "No, be a fucking adult and talk to him."

"He hates me!"

Brian rolled his eyes. "He doesn't hate you. Besides, that boy gets around."

I narrowed my eyes at him and shut the lid of my laptop. "What do you mean by that?"

"Nothing," he said too quickly.

"Bri!"

He sighed. "Not my business, but yeah, I've heard shit about him. He never wants any strings."

Hmm.

"He was kind of rude to me today."

"Well, you did stomp on his heart and then pretend he didn't exist for over a decade."

I sighed. "I know. I guess I have to go over there and ask him to hand back the password for the website."

"Yeah, you should."

I gave him a pleading look. "You sure you can't do it for me?"

"Be an adult and do it yourself. Maybe it will help you bury the hatchet."

I chewed on my lip. I highly doubted that. "Fine, you're the worst."

He grinned. "You love me."

"Hardly!" I said and stood up to leave.

It was around dinnertime, so it might be a bad time to go to the brewery. But that meant it could be a quick in-and-out visit. I told my parents I had to run an errand and walked over as if my feet were in molasses, dreading having to look into the eyes of the man I still loved but had to let go of.

As expected, the brewery was slammed. The tiny brunette girl who stood at the host stand looked frazzled as I walked up. "Do you want a table? It's gonna be a long wait."

I shook my head. "Is Declan around? I need to talk to him about something."

"Okay...who are you? Let me ask if he has time."

"Lila. Lila Sullivan."

"Gimme a minute."

She left to go into the back, and I spied her in the hallway next to the bathrooms, talking to Declan. We locked eyes and he nodded at me, but he didn't seem happy to see me.

I walked back toward where they stood, and the brunette girl rushed back to the host stand. I felt bad for interrupting her when they looked so busy. Declan walked away, and I followed him into the back office. Inside, there were two desks in the big office. Declan took a seat behind one and I sat in the chair he had across from it.

He rubbed a hand across his jaw. "Look, can I apologize for earlier?"

"Oh. That's okay. I deserved that."

"No, you didn't."

I looked down at my boots. "I do. I'm surprised you even agreed to speak to me."

"What's up?"

"Gemma suggested we update the website, but you still have admin access, so I wanted to get that back."

He nodded and took out a sticky note and wrote something on it. "Yeah, that's fine. I always help your dad when he needs it. I don't mind."

"Why did you tell Gemma she had to help us?" I blurted out.

His face reddened in embarrassment. "She wasn't supposed to tell you that."

I laughed. "I like her."

"I like her too, even if she's a huge pain in my ass. But she's family."

I gave him a quizzical look.

"Oh, right, you don't know. Gemma's sister Avery is Nol's new wife."

Oh. That would explain their sibling-like relationship.

"Is that all you needed?" he asked.

I nodded. "Yes. Thanks again, Dec. You didn't need to help us."

He put his glasses on and looked at his computer, promptly dismissing me.

I took the sticky note he slid over to me, but I didn't want to leave yet. My heart was doing somersaults looking at him. This was why I never wanted to come home after we broke up. I may have crushed his heart, but I also crushed my own.

"Congratulations, by the way," he muttered, but he wasn't looking at me.

"On what?"

"Aren't you getting married?"

A sob bubbled up in my throat, but I pushed it down. "No," I choked out.

"Lila?"

"He cheated on me. With his secretary," I hissed out.

A dark shadow cast across Declan's face, and I didn't miss the way his hands curled into fists. "I'm sorry. He sounds like an asshole."

I nodded. "I better go. Thanks, Dec. I really appreciate everything you've done for my family."

"I know how much the bar means to your dad. It would be a shame if it closed down."

He turned back to his computer, dismissing me and telling me exactly how he felt about me.

I walked out of his office without another word. The brewery was hopping, and as much as I wanted a drink, I needed to get out of there. This town was making all the feelings I didn't want to deal with come back to the surface.

I still loved Declan.

Oh god, after all these years, I still loved him, but we were so different now. I didn't know how to feel about him helping my parents after all the heartbreak I put him through. After tossing his heart into a blender and throwing our lifelong friendship away.

Instead of walking back to the bar, I got into my rental car and drove to my sister's house. Kelsey would be home from work by now and getting the kids' dinner together, and I needed to talk to her.

I knocked on the door, and she gave me a sympathetic

look when she opened it moments later. "Oh, honey, come in."

Then I burst into tears. "Crap, I'm sorry."

She gestured for me to come inside. "The kids just ate. You want something?"

"A beer."

I followed her into the kitchen and made a face when she gave me a Drake Pumpkin Ale. I took it anyway and got mad at how good it was.

Kelsey laughed at me. "Are you gonna tell me what's going on with you now?"

I sighed and slumped into her kitchen chair. She went to the stove and started fixing me a grilled cheese, because my sister was nothing if not a caregiver.

"Chad cheated on me."

"Dick!" she exclaimed as she flipped my sandwich.

"Yup."

"Is that why you came running when Mom called?"

I took another sip of my beer. "Yeah. You know what's the worst part?"

She continued cooking, flipping the grilled cheese again and holding the spatula in her hand. "What's that?"

"We haven't had sex in like five months."

Kelsey looked back at me in shock. "Really? I would be dying. Bri can't get enough of me, and me him. Well...that's the hormones."

I eyed her and then jumped up and hugged her. "Wait, is that how you're gonna tell me you're pregnant again?"

She laughed. "Yup. We weren't trying, but you know Bri, he's one of five. It must be genetics."

I laughed and hugged her again. "I'm so happy for you!"

"Sit down. You're making me nauseous."

I did as she asked and took another sip of my beer.

Damn the MacGregors for making such a good beer. I wanted to be mad about it, and annoyed that Declan still helped my family even though I tore apart his heart, but I couldn't be. It meant a lot that, despite it all, he still cared about my family. Even if he probably had a dartboard with my photo on it.

"When do you go back to work?" Kelsey asked, pulling me out of my drifting thoughts.

I let her question hang in the air while she finished making my sandwich.

"Lila?"

"I quit."

"What?"

"I quit and told Chad to get his stuff out of my house. When Mom called about Dad wanting to sell, I knew I needed to come back until the bar was settled."

She put the grilled cheese on a plate and brought it to me. I ate it silently while she made herself her own sandwich.

Kelsey fixed me with a look. "So, what's your plan?"

"Not sure. I had to go get the web admin password from Declan, so that was awesome," I muttered with a hint of sarcasm.

She cringed.

"Yup. And Gemma said we can share the table with them at the Harvest Fest this weekend."

Her eyes lit up. "Really? Gem mentioned that to me. That's awesome."

I nodded. Gemma seemed nice... excitable, but she knew what she was doing when it came to marketing. I wished I could hire her instead of sifting through freelance sites looking for someone that could help.

"Are you going to apply for a new job in the meantime?" my sister asked.

My lack of employment wasn't an enormous concern. I had a healthy savings account, so I'd be fine for a while. Saving the family bar was more important to me.

I waved her off. "I'll have no problem finding something, but I'm not sure I want to work in tech anymore."

"What do you want to do?"

"I want to save the bar," I blurted.

"Okay, but you're doing that already. Then what?"

I cocked my head at her. "Dad wants to sell. But what if he sells it to me?"

"Brian wanted to buy it, but we can't afford it. You know how much we love the bar and want it to stay in the family. But what's the plan? You buy it and go back to California?"

I took a sip of my beer in thought.

"I miss Philly," I admitted. "I miss Mom and Dad, and being a part of your lives."

My sister looked at me with her mouth agape. "Sis, I would love for you to come home for good, and Mom would be over the moon, but you need to think about this. You have a solid career and made a name for yourself as an IP lawyer out in California. You're upset about your breakup and not thinking straight."

I was upset about Chad cheating on me by fucking his secretary on his desk. Like, who does that? But I wasn't upset that we broke up, and he hadn't seemed like he was either. I was just upset he made a fool out of me.

I hadn't been happy in my career for a long time, and maybe a change of scenery was a good plan. I could easily land at another firm here in Philly. I'd have to pass the

Pennsylvania bar first, of course, but I could handle it. It wouldn't be tech money, but that wasn't important to me.

Kelsey patted my hand. "You think about it, don't make any rash decisions. Your life's in California, not here."

That was the thing she didn't get. I didn't have a life. You didn't have time for friends when you worked eighty-plus hours a week in a high-demanding field. Which was why I ended up dating the CEO of the tech company I was in-house counsel for. I spent all my waking hours in that office and barely any time at the large home I bought with all the money I made. I hadn't taken a vacation in three years.

The thing I wasn't telling my sister, and could barely admit to myself, was that I wasn't sure I wanted to be a lawyer anymore. But I was too young to have a midlife crisis, so I kept my mouth shut.

"Okay. I'll think about it, but I'm staying until Dad agrees not to sell the bar," I said.

Kelsey smiled at me. "Don't get me wrong, I'm glad you're home, but no one's asking you to sacrifice your career for the bar. We'll figure it out."

CHAPTER SIX

DECLAN

"Oh my god, will you go!" Wyatt huffed.

I rolled my eyes at him as I recounted the bills and put them back into the lockbox. Wyatt was holding onto the tablet we used for credit cards, but a lot of people still used cash at these events, so I always made sure we were prepared.

It had been a couple of days since I saw Lila, and I hoped she wouldn't show up at the Harvest Fest. Brian Murphy and Sean Sullivan had been beside us all day, dishing out traditional Irish food and promoting their bar. There had been no sign of Lila, and I was hoping not to have another run-in with her. I was a dick to her the last time we saw each other. I wished that old hurt hadn't stayed with me, but looking at her without wanting to imagine what it would be like to have her lips on mine again was hard.

Gemma bounced over to us. She really worked her magic at getting us a booth at the fest this year. I didn't care how she did it because it would help us be more visible. I went over numbers with our lead sales guy this week, and sales were doing well. The pumpkin beer and the new Oktoberfest beer were pulling their weight. I was glad Nolan made the pumpkin beer for Avery last year. People loved it, especially around this time of year. I loved when the numbers proved me wrong.

"Let me take over," Gemma said to me.

I shook my head. "Nope. That's not your job anymore."

She rolled her eyes and twirled her finger around a strand of pink hair. "But it's not yours either. Let me give you a break until Felix gets here."

The only reason I was manning the booth with Wyatt was that we ran out of pumpkin beer, so Felix ran back to the brewery to grab another keg. We still had the Oktoberfest beer, so we weren't sold out, but people had been guzzling the pumpkin beer.

As I stared up at the Ferris wheel, my mind went back to all the times in high school when Lila and I ran each other ragged, trying to get on as many rides as we could. I had been so fearless back then, not caring that all the rides arrived in suitcases. I wasn't so sure I wanted to partake in any of that now.

A commotion pulled me away from my thoughts. I looked up and saw Kelsey Sullivan with her toddler in her arms. Lila was walking behind her, holding the hand of Kelsey's other daughter. Cora was maybe six, and for a moment, I thought about all those times in high school when I thought that would have been my future with Lila. Brian reached for his little one, and she jumped into her daddy's arms. Watching all the men in my life become fathers sent a wave of jealousy through me.

Gemma peered at me curiously. "What's with you?"

"Nothing," I muttered. "I'm gonna go walk around and get some air."

She narrowed her eyes. "We're already outside."

I didn't answer her, but walked away.

I needed to get away from my ex-girlfriend. I wanted her family's bar to succeed, so I didn't mind helping them, but it didn't mean I wanted to see her. Her dad still checked in on me from time to time because he was a good guy, but being around her hurt. I wished it didn't. I was freaking thirty-four years old! I shouldn't still be hung up on the girl I dated as a teenager.

I walked through the fairgrounds and bumped into my brother. He had Norah strapped to his chest and was talking to Kelly Sullivan while Avery stood next to him drinking a cup of coffee. It seemed like I couldn't escape the Sullivans lately.

Kelly's eyes lit up when she saw me. "Declan!" she greeted me and gripped me in a big hug.

I hugged her back. "Hey, Mrs. Sullivan."

She made a face. "Honey, you know you can call me Kelly."

I shook my head. That was so weird. I spent most of my life calling her Mrs. Sullivan because Mom had trained me that was proper. I couldn't start calling her Kelly now.

Norah reached out toward me, and I smiled at my niece. I extended my hand, and she grabbed my finger in her tiny fist.

"Aw, so cute. When are you gonna have one of your own?" Kelly asked.

Nolan and Avery pinned me with very interested looks. That was the second time Kelly had asked me that recently.

"Yeah, Dec. When are you?" Avery asked.

Nolan rolled his eyes. "He's holding out for Lila."

I glared at him.

Kelly's smile got brighter. "She'll come around, hon."

I ran a hand down my face. "Um. Yeah, that's...we dated in high school, that's not why. I just haven't found the one yet."

Kelly beamed at me. "You will, one day. I better go check out the booth and see what my husband has forgotten. Avery, Nolan, congratulations, she's so cute."

Nolan puffed out his chest in pride, and Avery had a sly smile across her face. Kelly grabbed Avery's hand. "Norah would have loved you. It's clear you make Nolan very happy, and that's all she would have wanted."

"Thank you," Avery whispered.

When Kelly walked off, I pinned a glare at my big brother. "Asshole."

He scowled back at me. "Don't swear in front of my baby!"

"She can't even talk yet!" I argued.

Avery laughed into her paper coffee cup.

Nolan scowled, but Avery leaned up on her tip-toes, and he bent down to meet her in a gentle kiss. Avery had him wrapped around her little finger. It wasn't even funny.

Avery turned to me. "Is it true, though? Are you holding out for her?"

I shook my head. "Nah. That's the past."

Avery pursed her lips. "So why did Gemma text me asking why you literally ran away when Lila showed up?"

I clenched my teeth together. Fucking Gemma, such a tattle tell.

Avery laughed. "Just kidding, she didn't, but you looked annoyed when you came over. Wasn't that hard to figure out why."

"How's the booth doing?" Nolan asked.

"Fine, but we already ran out of pumpkin beer, so I sent Felix back to get another keg," I told him.

Nolan bounced Norah against his chest, slowly rocking her to sleep. "Do you think we need to go get more than that?"

"I told Felix to grab whatever else we had ready. We'll be fine. Enjoy your day off with your family," I told him sternly.

Avery cocked her head at me. "Declan, you're all about work-life balance, which is great because I love to see my husband, but do you ever take a day off?"

No. I didn't. Better to bury myself in managing the brewery than lie awake wondering why I was still alone.

It wasn't like I didn't get laid. I did. I just hadn't in a couple months. I was aware I had a reputation for a 'good time, not a long time.' I didn't ask for that reputation, but I never clicked with anyone since Lila.

"Brewery's too busy," I said.

Avery looked at Nolan and then back at me. "You two need to knock that shit off. Everyone needs a break."

"Okay, Mom," I said with a roll of my eyes.

Nolan gave me an annoyed look. "You've been hanging around Gemma too much."

I ran a hand across my jaw in annoyance. I deserved that after giving him so much shit when he wouldn't tell Avery how he felt about her.

Norah started to fuss, and she let out a loud wail. Nolan sighed. "We need to get this one home. Take the rest of the day off. I told Gemma she's in charge."

I glared at him. "Really?"

He nodded. "Gemma's excitable, but she knows what needs to be done. Go enjoy the fest. You used to love it."

Yeah, I used to love it because Lila loved it.

Avery gave me a small smile. "Dec, go take a day off already. You deserve it!"

I grumbled as I watched them walk away.

Avery wasn't wrong, but I felt like there was still so much I needed to get done. When Nolan worried about money last year after he found out Avery was pregnant, I did a lot to reassure him we were fine. We were, but I had those same worries.

I walked around the grounds, lost in thought, mostly because I didn't want to run into Lila again. I was being immature. I knew that. I should be an adult and deal with her. It wasn't like she ever stuck around.

I grabbed a hot dog from one of the food stands and peered up at the rickety carnival rides. Man, I couldn't believe we went on all of those over the years. Being older and wiser now, these suitcase rides were scary.

"Hey, Declan!" a high-pitched feminine voice called out to me.

Oh, good god, no.

Annie.

Annie bounced over to me. She was wearing a shirt way too tight for me not to notice her boobs, especially with that plunging neckline. I was a guy, so sue me if I looked. She wasn't supposed to be working the booth today, and I was hoping not to run into her.

She gave me a seductive smile and ran a finger down my chest before I could stop her. "What brings you here?"

I shifted away from her touch. I had done nothing but spurn her advances, and it wasn't clicking with her. It wasn't like she was unattractive, and she was a great girl, but I didn't date employees. Not anymore.

"Hey, Annie. How are you?" I asked stiffly, stepping a couple feet away.

"Good, now that you're here." She reached out and gave my bicep a squeeze. "Have you been working out? Your arms are looking so big!"

What the fuck?

Did she think that would stroke my ego or some shit?

I wasn't the type of guy women noticed as being in peak physical shape. I barely had any fat on my body, but that was more because of weird genetics than anything else. Whereas Nolan got Dad's big husky build, I was lanky and tall like Mom had been. No woman ever asked me if I was working out. Most women told me cuddling with me sucked because I was too bony.

"Um, no." I scratched my jaw, annoyed with the itchiness of my facial hair already coming in. "Look, Annie—"

"Hey, babe!" a familiar voice called out to me and cut off the rejection I was about to lay at Annie's feet.

I turned and saw Lila walking over to us with a big thing of cotton candy in her hand. A smile curled up on my lips at the memory of all the times she'd eaten too much of that when we were in high school. My girl loved her carnival food.

I shook my head at myself. Christ, she wasn't my girl anymore. I couldn't think like that.

My eyes trailed her up and down as she walked over. She wore a dark purple sweater that made her tits look fantastic with a black and white plaid skirt and knee-high black boots. I definitely wasn't thinking about her long legs wrapped around my waist while I fucked her in those boots. Definitely not.

Annie gave me a quizzical look, but Lila smiled at me as she came over to me and linked her arm with mine. "There you are," she said, and her hazel eyes told me to play along. "Sorry, the line was so long." She pulled off a piece of cotton candy and held it up to my mouth. I opened my lips and let her feed it to me.

Lila looked at Annie, whose face had settled into a hard line. Lila held out her hand to Annie. "Hi, I'm Declan's girlfriend, Lila. I don't think we've met."

"Annie," the other woman said through gritted teeth and didn't take Lila's hand.

Lila shrugged it off and turned to me, giving me that puppy dog look she always used to when we had been dating. "Can you please take me on the Ferris wheel now? You can kiss me at the top again, like when we first fell in love."

Her words hit me in the chest, and I wondered if she was still play-acting or if her words rang true. When we were sixteen, I took her on the Ferris wheel and kissed her for the first time. After years of being in the friend zone, I finally had the courage to make a move on her.

"Please?" Lila begged.

My dick kicked at my zipper at the sound of her begging for something. I wanted her to beg for something else, but while she was on her knees with her hands tied behind her back.

Damn, I really need to get laid.

"Okay, fine," I relented. "See you around, Annie."

We walked off together for a few moments, neither of us saying a word. Lila ate her cotton candy and walked beside me like nothing had ever happened between us. Like I hadn't seen her in sixteen years and was still pining over her.

"Thanks for the save," I finally said after we reached the zipper ride.

Man, we used to ride that all the time.

The sun had dipped beneath the horizon, and all the

rides had turned their lights on. I had been wandering around the fields longer than I had realized.

Lila had tossed her trash away a couple of minutes ago, but she stood staring up at the ride. "You looked like you needed saving."

"Mmmhmm."

"She's pretty. Why aren't you interested?"

"I'm her boss."

Lila nodded. "That's a deal breaker for you?"

"It's backfired for me before."

"Me too."

I wanted to ask what that meant, but she got that wild look in her eyes, and I knew exactly what she was going to ask next before the words were out of her mouth.

CHAPTER SEVEN

LILA

"Come on the zipper with me!" I urged.

He squinted at me, then looked up at the carnival ride with suspicion. The Declan in high school would have grabbed my hand and told me, 'you only live once.' This adult-Declan was cautious. Or maybe we were just dumb in high school and didn't think about how dangerous rickety carnival rides were.

I always loved the Harvest Fest. It brought back a lot of memories. Like the one of my first kiss with Declan at the top of the Ferris wheel. Or my first sip of beer. Even that first puff of stinky weed. I got up to a lot of shenanigans here when I was a teenager. All with the clean-cut uptight man standing in front of me.

I shivered and wrapped my arms around myself. Sure, it was fall, but the air was getting chilly now that the sun had gone down. In hindsight, the sweater and plaid skirt weren't a good idea. I had been living in California for so long that I should have known better and wore a pair of leggings at least.

Declan's dark eyes seared across the length of my body like he remembered all the times he had stripped me out of my clothes. He always did like the knee-high boots I wore during the fall.

"You cold?" he asked.

I nodded. "Been in California too long."

He shed his zip-up hoodie and put it over my shoulders. "Here."

A memory of this exact scene played through my mind's eye. Of me not wearing proper attire because I wanted to dress cute for him and him giving me his jacket. But that was sixteen-year-old Declan and Lila; we weren't those people anymore.

"Dec..."

"Come on, love, let's go on the zipper," he said and took my hand.

I didn't question his slip up. The old pet name rolled off his tongue like it hadn't been sixteen years since I broke his heart. Like I hadn't stood in his driveway all those years ago and told him I got accepted to Stanford and wasn't going with him to Penn State. I told him I wanted to break up, because long-distance relationships never worked, but I'd always love him. That part had been true, was still true, but I never came back to him. I went to California and stayed there while he stayed in our gossipy small town and made a name for himself.

The pad of his thumb brushed against the back of my palm. "Love?"

"Right. Let's go on the zipper!" I said excitedly, pulling myself away from the trip down memory lane.

We walked over to the ride and waited in line for a few

minutes, but neither of us wanted to sever the connection of our hands. I wondered if he was thinking about all the times we had done this before. Of those times back in high school when he was the one dragging me toward the rides. Adult Declan was quiet and reserved, and I couldn't get a read on him. He wasn't the boy I fell in love with, but yet, at the same time, he was.

He led me into the cage and made sure I was seated before he slid in next to me. We pulled the lap bar down, and the ride operator clicked us in before shutting us inside the metal cage. We were pressed so close together, I felt his thigh against my own.

I didn't know why I did it, but I turned to him and found he was staring back at me intensely. He didn't jerk back when I brushed my lips against his. He threaded his hands through my hair, one of them gripping my neck possessively as he deepened the kiss. We kissed like we hadn't forgotten, like it hadn't been years since we were pressed together. We still fit so perfectly.

Then the ride lurched, and I pulled away to grab onto the handlebar above my head as we moved upwards. We screamed our heads off as our cage flipped us around. I held onto Declan's arm when the ride took us up to its full height and then brought us back down to the ground, all the while flipping us upside down in our cage.

I felt dizzy by the time we were back on the ground, and the ride operator opened the cage for us. Declan got out first, then offered me a hand when I stumbled out.

He studied me. "Okay, love?"

I could only nod.

My heart was doing somersaults, and it wasn't because I was motion sick from the ride. It was singing with the way this man still turned me inside out. But I couldn't get ideas like that. I didn't deserve him after what I did. Not after I had been such a coward and cut him out of my life.

I shoved my hands in my pockets as we walked off. All the rides were lit up bright and colorful against the dark October night sky. It reminded me of being a kid, of all the possibilities. It helped me forget that my fiancé cheated on me and my family's bar was about to go under.

Declan walked with me around the fairgrounds. I don't think he knew what to say about that kiss, either. I wanted to know if his lips on mine still felt the same way, or if I was just nostalgic for my high school sweetheart.

It felt the same. When we kissed, it was like the planets aligned, and I knew for sure why none of my relationships had panned out since. My heart belonged to Declan freaking MacGregor.

"Lila," Declan began.

I turned to him and watched him rub a frustrated hand down his jaw. His five o'clock shadow had come in, but it looked like the type of scruff that would hurt good when he rubbed it against my face. Or my thighs.

My phone vibrated in my pocket, and I pulled it out, noticing a text from my sister.

KELS: *Can Dec give you a ride home? Cora puked on the scrambler, so we gotta go.*

Dammit.

ME: *I'll ask.*

KELS: *K! You looked cozy. Maybe it's a good thing.*

I ignored that last part. How she even knew I was with him was a mystery to me.

Declan gave me a quizzical look. "Everything okay?"

I sighed. "No. My sister ditched me, and she was my ride."

"Oh. I can take you home."

"You don't have to. I'll call a car."

"Lila, it's fine. I'll take you home."

"Thank you," I muttered and looked down at my boots.

We were both pretending the kiss didn't happen. If it happened, that meant I had to deal with all these pent-up feelings. When Declan kissed me, a lightbulb had gone off. When other men kissed me, I convinced myself I loved them. Convinced myself I could find love again. But my heart would always belong to the tall, lanky man in front of me.

"Hey, I want to get some funnel cake!" I said, trying to ease the tension between us.

A smile tugged at the corner of his lips. "Okay, let's get you some funnel cake. I gotta go check on the booth to make sure Felix and Gemma don't need anything before they close up. I'll meet you over by the funnel cake stand."

I nodded and watched him go. Okay, I watched his ass go. He had a nice ass that filled out the pair of jeans he was wearing. Declan wasn't a big guy with lots of muscles or a six-pack, but that never bothered me. Dad used to call him beanpole in high school, and not much had changed.

I wrapped his hoodie around me and breathed in the woodsy scent of his cologne. I walked over to the funnel cake stand and bought myself a plate. I was half done with it when Declan walked over to find me.

A smile curled across his lips. "You almost demolished that."

I laughed and held up the paper plate. "Did you want any?"

He broke off a piece of what was left and popped it into his mouth. He reached up a hand and cupped my face. I thought he was going to kiss me again, but his thumb brushed across my bottom lip instead. "You had some powdered sugar on your lips."

I gave him a sheepish smile. "Thanks."

His hand lingered, and I imagined him sliding that big thumb of his into my mouth. I imagined myself sucking on it, a sign of what else I wanted to suck on.

Damn, I hadn't realized how not having sex with my fiancé made me a ball of arousal.

His brown eyes looked like he was thinking about it too, but then he pulled away. I gave him the rest of the funnel cake and he ate it slowly. I watched him lick the sugar off his fingers until it was all gone. That shouldn't be sexy. I shouldn't think about him licking something else off his fingers, but I was. I was letting my horny brain take over. My rational mind was flashing with bright 'DANGER' signs, but I pushed it away.

Declan threw out the plate and brushed his hands off on his jeans. I pulled a wet wipe out of my purse and handed it to him. He smiled in thanks as we used the wipes to get the excess residue off our fingers.

"Ready to go?" he asked.

I nodded.

We walked back to his car together, and my nerves bound up inside me. I wanted to kiss him again. I wanted to feel his lips on mine, to memorize the way his kiss made me feel like I was home again. But we couldn't go there. I couldn't open that up and hurt him again.

In the car, Declan didn't start the engine right away. "Lila?"

But as much as I told myself no, I couldn't help myself. I leaned over and kissed him. We crashed together, and I slid my tongue across the seam of his lips. He grabbed my hair in a fist and angled me the way he wanted as he took control. He kissed me like a man who knew what he wanted, and I kissed him back with the same ferociousness. I wanted him *bad*.

While our tongues tangled up, I slid my hand down his torso and pressed against his jeans. He was raging hard, and I wanted to do something about it. He didn't notice me undoing the top button of his jeans and sliding his zipper down while we got lost in each other.

When I pulled his cock out of his boxers, he pulled away, his hands still gripping my hair. "What do you think you're doing?" he snarled.

I whimpered at the pain on my scalp, but I liked it. I liked his rough hands on me when he kissed me. I liked the way he looked at me, like he wanted to swallow me whole. That's probably why I dipped my head down and licked the bead of moisture off the head of his cock.

"Fuck," he moaned when I gripped his shaft and slid him into my mouth.

It wouldn't have been the first time I gave him head in a car parked at these fairgrounds. But the last time we did this, we were teenagers. And I misremembered how big his dick was. I opened my mouth wider to fit him all inside.

"Such a naughty girl, huh?"

I slid my lips down his cock, sliding it in and out of my mouth slowly, trying to get it wet enough so I could take it down my throat.

I looked up at him while I pulled back and sucked on the head of his cock. I repositioned myself so I was on my hands and knees and bent over his lap while I sucked his cock. His hand trailed down my back and gave my ass a little squeeze before slipping beneath my skirt. Without warning, he pushed my panties to the side and pressed two thick fingers inside me.

I moaned around his cock as I adjusted to the sensation of his big fingers filling me up. I didn't need any foreplay. I was already soaked by the time I put his cock in my mouth. He always did that to me. Sucking his dick made me sopping wet back in high school, and surprisingly, time hadn't changed that.

"Such a naughty girl, you're already wet for me," he whispered.

He pumped his fingers inside me nice and slow and pressed his thumb against my clit, a place Chad never bothered to find. I moaned around his cock again.

Oh God, I was gonna come. I was giving my ex-boyfriend head in his car while he fingered me, and I was two seconds away from coming all over his magical fingers. They had to be magical, because he was the only person I ever came with. I thought something was wrong with me after I went to college. I thought all those men sucked in bed, but maybe Declan was the only one who could hit that button deep inside me.

That was depressing. Or maybe I was cursed to only come with the man I lost my virginity to, karma's way of getting back at me for breaking his heart.

I felt his cock twitch in my mouth. I started to pull off, but he pressed my head back down onto it, forcing me to take it all back inside. "If you want to be a naughty girl who gives me car head, you're gonna take it down your throat and swallow my cum. You hear me?" he growled.

He gripped my hair tightly, and the hand pressed deep inside my pussy slipped out. I whined at the loss of his fingers, but then he slapped my clit as if to demonstrate what would happen if I didn't obey.

Holy shit!

Declan MacGregor just growled at me and slapped my

clit. I'd only ever seen that in porn! I didn't know men did that in real life. Or that I would like it so much. This wasn't the Declan I lost my virginity to. That Declan had been a shy sixteen-year-old, who made sure we had lots of lube and foreplay. This Declan was rough and demanding. He was all man, and the part of me that liked being held down during sex appreciated the change.

He slid his fingers back inside me, and I moaned around his cock again when his deft digits curled up deep.

"You take it all. I should punish you for being so naughty, huh?" he purred.

I nodded on his cock, sliding him in and out faster as I felt his hips arch up to go deeper. His cock pulsed inside, and I knew he was close, but I kept going. Licking and sucking, doing my best to get him to come down my throat. Seconds later, he let out a long, low groan as he exploded into my mouth. I sucked it all down, enjoying every last drop of it. He pumped his fingers deep inside me at the same time, sending me over the edge of my own pleasure. But my cries were silenced because his dick was still in my mouth.

He stroked my hair and looked down at me while I slid his cock out of my mouth. He reached a hand down and stroked my bottom lip. "Such a naughty girl. Coming all over my fingers while my cock's down your throat."

I shouldn't like him calling me a naughty girl, but I did. I loved it. I wanted to be his naughty girl. I didn't know what sort of punishment he wanted to give to me, but it sounded exhilarating. Would he take me over his knee and spank me until I begged him to stop? Or would he face fuck me until I gagged on his cock again? Or maybe he'd tie me up for being so naughty. I liked all three possibilities. Chad never wanted to explore my fantasies. He tried once, but the cheap metal handcuffs had hurt too much, so we never tried it again. I only ever fulfilled those fantasies in the books I read, but never in my own bed.

Declan pulled his fingers from beneath my skirt, and I watched with my head still in his lap as he stuck his fingers in his mouth and sucked my cum off them. He did it one by one and closed his eyes as he tasted me for the first time in sixteen years.

"Fuck, that's hot," I blurted out.

"Not hotter than you deep throating me in my car. You okay, love?" He smiled down at me and lovingly stroked my scalp where he had pulled my hair. It was sweet of him to check in after the intense orgasm we both had.

I nodded and moved so I was no longer lying in his lap, but sitting in the passenger seat next to him. My panties were a ruined mess of cum, and my hair was a wreck, but I hadn't been that satisfied in a really long time.

No one had made me come like Declan MacGregor. Which was wild to think about. No one came with their high school boyfriend. The men you slept with after you lost your virginity usually knew what they were doing. But no one else knew me inside and out like the man who had been my best friend since the third grade.

Declan zipped his jeans back up and started the engine. I buckled myself into my seatbelt in the passenger seat as he drove off, neither of us speaking. I was too sexually satisfied to say anything, and all he did was finger me.

"I'm taking you home," he said after a few minutes had passed.

"Okay," I whispered.

"And then I'm gonna fuck you like you've never been fucked before."

Oh. He meant his place.

"Okay."

"Lila, tell me you want that."

I nodded.

"Say the words, love. I need to know you want this."

"Yes."

We didn't say anything else while he drove us back to Drakesville. This was a supremely bad idea, but my pussy had other ideas.

CHAPTER EIGHT

DECLAN

This was such a bad idea. I shouldn't take my ex-girlfriend back to my apartment to fuck her like the heathen I was, but my horny brain didn't care.

I had every intention of giving Lila a ride home and pretending she hadn't kissed me on the zipper. Then she had to kiss me again in my car, and when she bent down and took my cock in her mouth, it was all over.

I wanted to do so many things to her tonight. Like take her over my knee and spank her for breaking my heart. Or tie her up and punish her with too many orgasms until she was a puddle of satisfaction. I didn't think Lila was the type of woman who would agree to wrist restraints, no matter how much I wanted that.

I wasn't the same cautious guy when we were teenagers. I liked to be in control, especially in the bedroom. I wanted a woman who submitted to me. It felt like she was into that, since she didn't mind how rough I got with her in the car. But that could have been the heat of the moment.

I parked in my spot behind the tattoo shop, cut the engine, and looked at her for reassurance that she wanted to do this. She stared back at me wide-eyed, but then she nodded. I got out of the car and walked her around to the front of the building. She didn't ask questions when I opened the door next to the tattoo shop. We walked up the steps, and I unlocked and opened the door for her, letting her enter my apartment.

She shed my hoodie and laid it across the back of the couch while I shut and locked the door behind us. I stalked over to her, and she blinked up at me. "Declan?"

"Bedroom. Now," I growled.

She jumped at my demand, but walked toward the door on the other side of the apartment. She looked back at me in question, and when I nodded, she opened the door to my bedroom. Like the rest of my apartment, it was neat and tidy. My bed was made up, and everything was put away in its proper place. As it should be.

Lila stood in front of my bed, unsure what to do next. I walked inside and began unbuttoning my plaid shirt. I took that off, leaving me in a t-shirt. "Leave the boots on. Strip," I said.

I sat at the foot of the bed and tossed my t-shirt to the other side of the room. I'd put that in the hamper later. Lila turned around in front of me and pulled the sweater over her head. Beneath it, she wore a pale pink lacy bra that looked perfect against her sun-kissed skin. I undid my jeans and boxers and pushed them off while she slid her skirt down her ankles. She wore a matching pair of panties beneath the skirt. Panties I knew were soaked with cum already.

My dick stood at attention at the sight of her in just her bra and panties. I gripped my shaft and stroked it while I watched her undress. She licked her lips as she watched me touch myself.

"Look what you do to me," I said as I pumped my hand up and down.

She bit her lip, reaching behind her back and unclasping her bra. She let it fall to the floor, and I had to hold back at the sight of her gorgeous tits. Fuck, I had missed those tits. They were still so perky and perfect. I wanted to bury my face and my cock between them. I stroked harder and watched her slide her panties down her legs. My fingers had been inside that pussy in the car, but now I wanted my mouth on it. And then my cock buried deep inside, fucking her until she screamed my name.

She knelt on the floor and kissed my thighs, inching her lips up to my cock again. "What do you want to do to me?"

Her on her knees, inches from my cock, was a sight to behold, but the next time I came was going to be in her pussy. Not her mouth.

"I want you on the bed ready for me," I told her instead.

She did as I asked and laid back on the bed. She spread her legs wide and surprised me when she dipped a hand down between her legs. Holy shit, Lila Sullivan was naked in my bed and touching herself because she couldn't wait for me to do it. I squeezed my eyes shut and tried to hold off blowing my load. I wanted to watch her come apart beneath me before I gave into my own pleasure.

I stood up and kicked my discarded clothes away. I went around to the bedside table next to her. I took off my watch, laid it on the table, and opened the drawer, taking out a bottle of lube and a box of condoms.

I crawled on top of Lila and boxed her head in with my arms. She was still touching herself. I could hear the slick wetness of her pussy as her fingers stroked in and out fast and frantic, like I hadn't made her come already tonight. I pulled her hand away and lifted her fingers up to my lips. I sucked them into my mouth and moaned at the taste of her on my lips. She still tasted so sweet and perfect, and all mine.

At least for tonight.

I pressed her hands together above her head with one of my hands. "Such a naughty girl, starting without me."

She struggled against my grasp, but in a way that told me she liked it. Hmm, maybe I could ask about using the restraints tonight.

"Be a good girl for me, and I'll give you what you want," I whispered against her neck.

I pressed tiny kisses across her neck until I traveled to her lips and slanted my mouth on hers again. She mewed into the kiss as I held her down and took control. I kissed her hard and rough, and she thrashed against my hands while our tongues battled it out.

I trailed my lips down her jaw again and nuzzled my head into her luscious brown hair, breathing in the floral scent of her shampoo.

"What if I'm a naughty girl?" she asked.

"Then I'm gonna have to punish you," I whispered into her ear.

She whimpered. "Do it."

"Do you trust me?" I asked.

She nodded.

I reached into the bedside drawer and pulled out the wrist restraints. "You have a safe word?"

She bit her lip and thought for a moment. "Pumpkin."

We both laughed. This girl, who loved Halloween and whose favorite season was fall, would pick that as her safe word.

I held her arms above her head, undid the velcro around one cuff, and wrapped it around one of her wrists. I hooked a strap onto the metal ring on the cuff and tied that to my headboard. Then I repeated the action with her other wrist.

"Okay?" I asked.

She pulled on the restraints, testing their tightness, and then nodded. "What are you gonna do to me now?"

"Tease you," I purred as I pulled one of her legs up and pressed a tiny kiss on the inside of her thigh. "You look sexy as hell tied up in my bed naked except for these boots."

I kissed my way up to her hips, and when she arched up to get me to go where she wanted, I kissed the other thigh. She writhed around on the bed, and it turned me on how sexually frustrated she was. She probably would have tried to push my head toward her pussy if her hands weren't bound. I liked being in control, loving that I could torture her by going at my slow pace. This was so much better.

"Declan," she whined and wiggled her legs around to reach my mouth.

"Patience," I growled. "Or I'll tie your ankles up too, and then I'll play with you all night, not giving you the satisfaction you want."

"I'll be good," she stammered out.

Liar. She wanted to be at my mercy. I could tell from the arousal in her eyes, but maybe we'd do that next time. I had to warm her up to this first.

I kissed my way up her body again until I hefted one of her breasts in my hand. I bent my head down and flicked my tongue over her nipple. She pressed herself up into my mouth, trying desperately to get the pleasure she wanted from me. It was hot to watch how painfully turned on she was as she writhed around, desperate for me to give her the release she needed. But she had to play by my rules.

She rocked against her restraints, arching her body up against me, begging me to give her more. I pressed her back down against the bed and moved to her other breast, toying with her like I had all the time in the world.

"Declan," she groaned as if in pain and dug the heels of her boots into my back.

I lifted my head up from her breast. "Behave! Or I'll leave you wanting."

"Please, baby," she moaned, the desperation in her voice apparent. That made me want her even more.

"Not yet," I whispered and kissed my way back down her body.

I spread her legs wide and settled myself in between them. I pressed my thumb against her needy clit and looked up at her when I finally darted out my tongue across her slit. Her hips bucked up against the sensation of my tongue. I licked again, slower, torturing her a little while she whimpered and thrashed against the restraints.

I stopped licking her and gave her clit a little slap. "Behave, or you don't get anything," I snarled.

"Please, I need you," she whined.

I pressed two thick fingers inside her pussy, and her walls felt tight as I pumped them in and out. I couldn't wait to have my dick inside her, but I wanted her to beg for it. I wanted her to need me inside her so badly that she begged me to pound her pussy until I broke her. I smirked at her before I bent my head again and sucked her clit into my mouth.

"Oh, fuck," she moaned and arched up against my mouth.

Lila wasn't big on swearing back in high school. Either she changed or I was melting her brain with pleasure. I think it was the latter with the way she pulled against the restraints while I ate her pussy like I was a starved man. And I kind of was. Don't get me wrong, many women had been in my bed. Women who wanted a good time and the thrill of being tied up for the first time. But none of them were my Lila, and like her, none of them stayed.

I closed my eyes and enjoyed myself as I ate her out. Her cries of pleasure egged me on to press her further to the edge of ecstasy. My dick was a raging point against the bed, but all that mattered in this moment was that I gave her the pleasure she needed. She moaned so loudly that it made me finger her erratically and suck her clit harder.

"Yes, fuck!" she screamed.

Her legs shook like jelly as her orgasm washed over her, but I wasn't done with her yet. I kept licking and sucking until she came all over again. Until she screamed my name and rocked against the restraints above her head.

"Declan, baby, so good," she whimpered. "I need your cock. Please, please, please."

I slapped her clit again and nipped at her thigh. "You'll get it when I say you get it."

"Please," she begged as she looked down at me with a pleading look. So hot when they begged for it.

"Fine, I guess you've been good enough," I relented.

My resolve was slipping. Normally, I would have made her beg a little more, but when this woman looked at me, all my defenses came crashing down. Or maybe it was because I never thought I'd ever have her like this. In high school, we had boring vanilla sex because we were teenagers. I hadn't known that I liked certain things in bed yet.

I grabbed the condom from the bedside table, took it out of the package, and slipped it down my cock. Lila watched me hungrily when I slicked lube down my length. I pumped my dick in my hand a few times before spreading her legs again and plunging inside her tight pussy. She gasped at how quickly I buried myself inside her.

"Take it," I ordered.

She nodded and wrapped her boot-clad legs around my waist while I rolled my hips and took her hard. Her heels dug into my back, and I thrust harder. She pulled against the restraints, and I loved that she wanted to touch me, but she wasn't allowed to. That made it hotter.

"Naughty girl, that's why I had to tie you up," I purred and pressed my thumb against her clit.

She squeezed her legs around my waist tighter, and I grinned at her trying to skirt the rules. But we both knew I was in charge tonight.

"My rules, love," I said sternly.

"Your rules," she repeated, but she didn't stop squeezing my waist with her thighs.

"Be a good girl, and I'll give it to you hard like you want."

"What if I'm a bad girl?" she asked, biting her lip to test me. Like I wouldn't punish her for disobeying.

I slowed my pace, sliding in and out of her so slowly that it felt like torture for both of us. She whined at the unhurried pace. "I'll go that slow all night long. Beg me to go faster. Beg me to fuck you like the animal I am."

"Please, Declan. I'm your good girl. Please give it to me."

I quickened my pace, pressing deeper inside her, then sliding back out again. I repeated the action, slamming in and out of her like I couldn't get enough of her. She closed her eyes and ground her hips up to meet my every movement. We were in sync with each other as our bodies moved together like we were one entity. I clenched my jaw, knowing I was close to coming, but I wanted to get her there one last time.

I grabbed her face in my hands and looked deep into her hazel eyes. In the dim light of my bedroom, her golden eyes sparkled. When she looked at me, it was like she knew every part of my soul, inside and out.

"Come with me, my love," I whispered, more like begged her. I beseeched her to feel what I felt tonight. Old feelings were bubbling up to the surface, and it was hard to push them back down when she looked at me like she was mine.

She kissed me and squeezed her boot-clad legs around my waist tighter as she came. I was right behind her. I released her mouth to let out a low guttural groan as I came in long, hot spurts inside her. I came like I had never come before. Like I had been waiting for this woman, and this woman alone.

We were both out of breath but stayed joined for a moment while we came back down to earth. After a few more seconds went by, I pulled out of her and took the condom off, tossing it in the garbage. I undid the velcro of the cuffs above her head and released her from the restraints. I rubbed a hand across one of her wrists and kissed it softly. Then I repeated the action with her other wrist. I untied the straps from the bed and put the restraints back into the bedside drawer.

Lila laid back on the bed with a satisfied sigh. I leaned over and kissed her, putting every ounce of feeling into it. She wrapped her arms around me and stroked my hair while we kissed. Her lips on mine made me realize I felt nothing with any of those other women.

I broke off from her and stroked her wrists again. "You

okay?" I asked. I needed to check in to make sure I hadn't hurt her.

"I'm good," she breathed out.

I gave her another quick peck on the lips and then got off her to take a leak. When I opened the door to the bathroom when I was done, she was standing there still naked but without the boots. She leaned up and kissed me sweetly. It was like coming home, like sixteen years hadn't passed between us. I should have stopped it. I shouldn't have taken her home tonight, but my heart and my dick knew what they wanted, and my brain needed to stay out of it.

I let her go so she could go to the bathroom, and I walked back into my bedroom. I put my clothes into the hamper. My eyes twitched at the sight of her clothes strewn across the floor. So I folded those up and laid them on the chair next to my bed. I didn't like messes.

I got back into my bed and laid on my back.

Was it dumb to fuck her? Probably. Did I regret it? Absolutely not.

A moment later, Lila came back into the room and slid into the bed beside me, curling up against my chest. Other women said I was too pointy to cuddle with, but she never complained and wasn't doing that now. I wasn't the picture of masculinity. I was a lanky guy with skinny arms and legs, not a big beefy dude with six-pack abs. You could tell I spent a lot of my time behind a desk.

I kissed the top of her head and brought her wrists up to my lips again. One after the other. Aftercare after restraining a woman was important to me. "You sure you're okay, love?" I asked.

She nodded. "Yes."

"Was that your first time being restrained?"

She shook her head. "My ex did it once, but he used

metal handcuffs, and they cut into my skin. Those cuffs were comfortable. Thank you."

I stroked her hair while we cuddled together in my bed.

"That was different than before," she whispered while she laid her head on my chest and stroked her finger across my chest.

"We're not teenagers anymore," I said.

"True. I guess we both grew up a lot since I...since I left."

"Mmmhmm."

I kissed the back of her palm and noticed she still wore the Claddagh ring on her right hand. The ring depicted hands holding a heart with a crown on the top. The heart was facing away from her, meaning she was single. When I gave this to her, she wore it facing her to show she was mine.

"You still have this?" I asked as I kissed my way from the back of her palm to her wrist, soothing the spot where I had restrained her.

"I never take it off," she admitted.

"Oh."

I wasn't sure what to do with that information. Why would she never take off the ring I gave her back in high school? Why never speak to me again, but keep that ring?

We lay together in the dark of my bedroom in silence for a couple of moments. I stroked her hair gently while she laid across my chest, like she fit beside me.

"Declan?" she asked.

I kissed her forehead and lifted the comforter over our naked bodies. "Shush, love. Let's go to bed," I whispered.

She didn't fight or struggle against me. Instead, she laid back down, and we fell asleep in each other's arms.

CHAPTER NINE

LILA

I should go. I should quietly find my clothes and slip out while Declan was still asleep. But I didn't want to leave the comfort of his arms. Because he felt like home, and this was exactly why I avoided coming back to Drakesville. I knew if I saw him again, I would never leave. I would've let him and this town swallow me up, and I'd never have had the career I have now. Even if I was starting to question that career.

What did I have to show for it? I worked too many hours a week for a tech company that only saw me as a number. I've had countless failed relationships and two broken engagements. Chad wasn't the first person to put a ring on my finger, but it hadn't worked out the first time, either. The worst part? I didn't care when it was over. Sure, it hurt, but I hadn't been heartbroken over it.

Your high school boyfriend wasn't supposed to be the one. You weren't supposed to be hung up on him for the last sixteen years of your life. You certainly shouldn't have slept with him again.

"Love?" Declan whispered in the dark of his bedroom.

"I should go," I muttered and disentangled myself from his arms, but he flipped me onto my back and held my arms above my head, holding me in place.

"Stay," he said, but more like commanded it.

I hadn't expected Declan to be so dominating in bed. It made sense in high school we only ever had vanilla sex, but now, he was like all the fantasies come true. It was exhilarating when he told me to strip for him last night and then tied me to his bed to go at his pace. I had fought against the restraints, but that had been part of the fun.

"Stay," he repeated, and he nuzzled his face into my neck and kissed me.

I arched up into his touch, straining to escape his grasp, but it was all pretend, because I liked being held down. I wrapped my long legs around his waist and felt his dick harden against me.

"Declan," I moaned as he sucked on my flesh.

"Can I get you to stay now?"

He cupped my face and stared into my soul. I wanted to go, but I wanted him again. I wanted to be with the only man who had ever made me come again. Even though I'd slip out when he fell asleep, and avoid him for the rest of my life. All those old feelings were bubbling up to the surface, and my heart told me to stay for good, to stay for him. But I couldn't. That didn't stop me from giving in to his touch again.

I nodded at his question, and when he kissed me again, my heart sang. It reminded me that no one else ever made me feel like he did. That this man was my soulmate, and he had kept my heart under lock and key since the moment I shredded his all those years ago.

"Hands and knees," Declan said when he pulled away from the kiss.

I did as he commanded. I would let him do anything he wanted to me tonight. I loved the growly voice he used in bed and how he ordered me around. Declan was a gentleman in the streets but a Dom in the sheets, and I loved it.

He gently pushed my hair off my shoulder and pressed a kiss to it. "You're mine tonight."

I nodded, keeping my head facing the bed, while behind me, he ran his hands down my body. He gave my ass a little slap. "You got that, love?"

"Yes. Make me yours."

"Good girl," he purred.

I heard the bedside table open and the sound of him opening a condom wrapper and then the bottle of lube. He might be demanding in bed, but he still was a considerate lover who used lube. I loved that about him. Most men barely knew to do foreplay, but not him.

He took something else out of the drawer, and then he pulled my arms behind my back. I fell face-first onto the bed, and he bound my hands behind my back with padded leather handcuffs. Unlike the wrist restraints we used earlier, they had a chain linking them together, making them harder to get out of. I couldn't see what they looked like, but they definitely weren't velcro like the other pair.

It was always the quiet ones you had to watch out for. I never expected this from Declan, but I was wet already at the thought of him fucking me from behind as I lay helpless and bound.

He lifted my hips up in the air, pressing his groin

against my ass. He ran the head of his cock across my slit, and I moaned and pushed back at him, trying to get him to plunge inside me sooner. The crack of his hand on my ass bounced across the room.

"Naughty girl, you have to wait," he snarled, digging his hands into my hips.

"Please, Declan. I need your big cock inside me now," I begged.

"Wait," he ordered as he played with me some more.

He ran the head of his cock across my clit, and I moaned at the sensation. He wasn't even inside me yet, but waves of pleasure were building up already. I was in his complete control, and I had to play by his rules.

"Pumpkin," I said into the bed as a test.

He stopped and turned my head so he could look into my eyes. "Do you want to stop?"

I shook my head. "No."

"Then what's wrong?"

"I wanted to know...if you would stop."

He gave me a quick gentle kiss. "Lila, if you say your safe word, I'll stop doing whatever I'm doing. I'm serious. If you're not okay with me being dominant, tell me."

I shook my head. "No, I like it."

A smile curled up on his lips, and he gripped my jaw tight. "You were testing me, huh?"

I nodded.

"Okay, now?" he asked. He searched my eyes, looking for consent, checking in with me to make sure I wanted this too. He could be dominant, but he was still my sweet Declan. He'd never do anything to hurt me. Unless I asked.

I nodded again.

He turned me back around and pressed my face into the pillow. Then he groaned as he buried himself to the hilt.

"Fuck, yes," he growled out as he slid his cock in and out of me, taking me hard as I was helpless beneath him. I loved that he bound my hands behind my back and pressed me into the mattress as he fucked me from behind.

"You love being tied up, don't you?" he asked.

He was so rough in bed; it was so unexpected and made pleasure rise inside me. I was on the cusp of coming. I arched my ass back into him, trying to get better leverage as he pressed deeper inside until he bottomed out. Until he filled me up as far as he could go.

"Tell me you love being at my mercy," he commanded.

"I love it."

"You love being punished by my big dick."

"I love your big dick. The only dick that's ever made me come," I moaned in confession.

I didn't want him to know that, but I lost myself in the feeling of him. In being bound and laid out like a meal for him.

He rolled his hips, and I pressed back into him again. I thought he'd punish me for trying to meet him, but as our bodies writhed together, he slipped a hand down and found my clit. I came so hard; I forgot my own name.

His soothing voice in my ear brought me back. "That's a good girl. You like when I fuck you into the mattress, huh?"

"Mmmhmm," I moaned as I came down from the orgasm, but he didn't stop. He went rougher, pounding my pussy until we came together in loud guttural screams as lust poured out of us.

I laid my head on the pillow in defeat while Declan pulled out and tossed the condom in the trash. He undid the cuffs on my wrists and then kissed them again before putting the cuffs back into the drawer. I wondered what else he had in that drawer of his.

He pulled me into his arms again and wrapped the comforter around our naked bodies. "Stay," he said.

A part of me wondered if he was just saying for tonight. Or if he was begging me to stay in Drakesville for good.

"Please, love."

I nodded. "Okay."

🍁

But I left.

After he fucked me two more times, we passed out in each other's arms at three in the morning. I didn't know where he got the stamina, but it gave us this night together. Because that was all it was. One night to satisfy our lust.

I slipped out of his bed as quietly as I could in the morning, careful not to wake him. I put my clothes back on and cursed when I saw all the texts from my parents and my sister. I should have stayed at Kelsey's instead of Mom and Dad's. Even though I was thirty-four years old, my mom still badgered me about when I was getting home. Not telling her where I went meant I was going to deal with some passive-aggressive Irish mother stuff when I got home. It was close to noon, and I never set an alarm last night because I wasn't supposed to stay over.

I walked down the steps, and when I stepped outside, I bumped into Lizzie, who was opening the tattoo shop. She gave me a once over and arched an eyebrow at me. Her lavender hair was up in a messy bun, and she had the biggest smirk on her face.

Crap. Of course she would catch me doing the walk of shame as I left Declan's.

"Shut it!" I exclaimed.

She laughed. "I didn't say anything!"

"Not a word! I gotta go," I said and started walking away.

"Gimme the deets later!" she called after me.

I rolled my eyes and walked down the street.

My rental car was still at my parents' house, but luckily they lived closer than Kelsey did. Declan and I became fast friends in elementary school because I lived down the street from him, and our parents had been best friends. It was one of the reasons it had been so particularly hard to let him go.

Once I got to my parents' house, I'd tell them I wasn't dead, and then I'd head over to Kelsey's. I told her I'd go with her to the farm up in Buckingham to pick pumpkins with the girls today. Maybe even talk Kelsey into letting me carve them with Cora. Cora loved Halloween as much as I did, and she had been begging me to stay to take her trick or treating. But, it was only the second of October, and I couldn't make that promise.

I sighed when I walked up to my parents' driveway and saw my sister's car parked on the street outside. I was in big trouble.

I opened the door, and it was like all eyes were on me.

"Well, look who it is!" Kelsey teased.

Mom came out of the kitchen with her hands on her hips. "Where have you been, young lady?"

"Mom, relax. I'm thirty-four," I said with a roll of my eyes.

She glared at me. "Well, how did I know you weren't dead in a ditch?"

"I left her carless at the Harvest Fest," Kelsey cut in. "She was supposed to get a ride home from Declan MacGregor."

Mom's deposition immediately shifted, and she had a

big smile on her face. "Oh, well, why didn't you say you were at Declan's? You had me worried."

I sighed. "Can someone give me coffee?"

Kelsey held up a Wawa to-go cup. Oh my god, I missed Wawa coffee! I took the coffee from her and sipped it. I felt hungover, but then I realized I was just old and tired because I barely got any sleep last night. Damn Declan and that amazing dick of his.

"You ready?" Kelsey asked.

"Gimme a minute. I need to change."

She grinned at me. I wasn't surprised when she followed me upstairs into my childhood bedroom. I shrugged off my boots and looked through my suitcase. I found a pair of jeans and a long-sleeved black shirt.

My sister sat on the bed and waited impatiently for me to say something while I changed. I went to take off my underwear, when I remembered I couldn't find them this morning.

"Shit."

"What's up?"

I grimaced. "Forgot my underwear."

She laughed. "So, are you going to tell me about it?"

I shook my head, put on a new pair of panties, and changed out of my skirt into jeans.

"Why? Was it bad?" she asked.

"God, no. It was amazing. You know how I have trouble...you know..."

I felt heat rise up on my cheeks. I wasn't comfortable talking about this, but my sister had no shame about telling me sometimes you had to train men, like she did with Brian. I didn't need to know that, but Kelsey had no filter.

"Coming?" she asked.

"Yeah. Not actually the case."

Her face lit up. "Shut your face! Only he can do it?"

I grimaced and changed my shirt. I sipped on my coffee. "I thought something was wrong with me."

Kelsey snorted. "Nah. I thought you had really bad taste in men. I figured Declan was vanilla in bed, though. He's all nice and orderly."

My face colored at the thought of all the stuff we did last night. Declan was not vanilla. It wasn't like he was a Dom with a sex dungeon or anything, but a guy with wrist restraints and a separate set of leather handcuffs wasn't any shade of vanilla.

"Can we go?"

"No, tell me more!" she begged.

"Later!"

"Party pooper!"

"You're the one who asked me to go with you and the kids to get pumpkins!"

"Yeah, but now I want to know about what happened with you and Declan."

I shrugged. "It was just sex. Nothing else. Can we go?"

We walked down the steps and my niece Cora ran to me. "Auntie Lila!"

"Hey, kiddo. Wanna go pick out pumpkins?"

"I'm gonna pick the biggest one you've ever seen!"

I laughed and let her lead me out to the car. My sister glared as we said goodbye to Mom, telling me our conversation wasn't over.

CHAPTER TEN

DECLAN

She was gone in the morning, and I couldn't say I was surprised, but it still hurt. She was so pliable last night, so into wanting to submit to me. Being with her had all those old feelings swarming back.

I should go to the brewery and forget about last night. I should chalk it up to it being a one-night stand. We were just nostalgic for high school and wanted to be in each other's arms one last time. But that didn't stop me from getting up and going to her parents' house.

Kelly Sullivan opened the door a second after I knocked, and her face lit up when she saw me. "Declan! What do I owe the pleasure?"

"Hey, Mrs. Sullivan. Is Lila around?"

"She and Kelsey took the girls to the farm to pick pumpkins. You just missed her."

I sighed. "Right. The one up in Buckingham?"

She smiled at the fact I remembered. Every year we

went to the farm around this time. We'd pick pumpkins, get lost in the corn maze, and take the hayride. When we got older, it was just me and Lila; she always wanted to bring the biggest pumpkin home to carve.

"That's the one!" Kelly said.

"Thanks, Mrs. Sullivan."

She put her hand on my arm. "Declan, honey, she'll come around. She'll realize that she made a mistake breaking up with you. But no matter what, we still consider you family."

"Thanks, Mrs. Sullivan."

When I was walking home, I realized if I was going after her; I needed coverage at the brewery. I shot off a text to my brother.

ME: *Gotta take the day to take care of something. You good?*

NOLAN: *Bro, weren't you the one yelling at me to take time when Avery was pregnant? Take a day off.*

I shoved my phone back into my pocket and walked around the back of my apartment building to my car. I wasn't sure why I was going after her when I knew we didn't have a future together. But my body ached and my heart wrenched for her. I was hopeless.

It was about a half-hour drive to the farm. Did I think about turning back and going to the brewery instead? Yup. But I didn't because my heart and my dick were in control today. Last night, it was like we fell back into place, like we were teenagers again, without a care in the world. But we were thirty-four, and for some reason, I was chasing the woman who got away.

I parked my car on the lawn, took my glasses off, and rubbed the bridge of my nose. Was I making the right choice here? What was I doing? I wasn't sure what I would say to her when I saw her.

But my heart told my brain to get out of the car and go find her. I let it do all the thinking for me as I walked toward the entrance and paid for my admission. I took the hayride over to the patch where all the big pumpkins were and almost stopped in my tracks when I saw her with her toddler niece on her hip. Callie had that vibrant Celtic red hair she got from both sides of her family, looking like a little clone of Kelsey. Lila had beautiful chestnut-colored hair from Kelly, but I noticed her in a sea of people.

I strode over to them, and Lila jumped when she turned around and saw me. Callie held onto Lila's neck when she saw me. Lila held her niece closer to her chest. "It's okay, sweetie. It's just Declan. You know Declan."

"Hi," I said.

Lila raised an eyebrow at me. "Um. Hi."

"Your mom said you were here."

"Declan!" Kelsey called out and walked over to us with her other daughter holding her hand. The other little one was carrying a pumpkin that looked bigger than her.

"Whoa, there. That's a big pumpkin," I said to Cora.

Cora beamed at me. "I picked it myself."

Kelsey grimaced as she looked around frantically for something. For what, I wasn't sure. She gave her sister a pained look. "Can you watch the kids?" Lila nodded, and Kelsey looked at her daughters. "Stay with Auntie Lila."

"What's wrong with mommy?" Cora asked.

I looked over and watched Kelsey find a trash can and throw up in it.

Oh.

I turned back to Lila and gave her a questioning look, and she nodded at my silent question.

"Baby," Callie muttered to Lila.

Lila's eyes widened, but she deflected. "You the baby."

"I'm baby," Callie repeated.

Lila looked at Cora. "Cora, say hello to Declan."

Cora waved at me, but she seemed more fascinated by her pumpkin. It looked pretty big for her. I bent down in front of her. "You want me to carry that for you?"

She hugged her pumpkin tighter and shook her head fiercely. "I'm a big girl."

"Okay, kiddo."

I stood up to my full height, and then Kelsey came back over to us. She took Callie out of Lila's arms and handed the kids apple cider donuts. She looked at me. "Fancy seeing you here." She gave her sister a look.

Lila nodded. "Gimme a minute."

Kelsey nodded, and Lila led me away from her family. We walked along the path of the pumpkin patch in silence for a couple of moments. All the while, I was itching to hold her hand. Like I was a freaking teenager again.

She stopped and turned to me with a confused look on her face. "What are you doing here?"

"You left."

She nodded. "I...I'm sorry."

I took my glasses off and wiped them clean with my t-shirt. I put them back on my face, and she smiled at me. I wasn't sure why, because she looked pissed off at me a second ago. "I don't know why I came here."

"Okay..."

"Last night was amazing."

A blush crept up her face. "I had a good time."

"I wanted you to be there this morning, and it pissed me off that you snuck out when I was asleep."

She nodded. "I'm sorry, that was shitty of me. Declan, I'm not here to stay. It would be unfair of me if we—"

"How long are you in town for?"

She shrugged.

I gave her a suspicious look. "You have to go back to work, right?"

She looked down at her feet and twirled a strand of hair between her fingers. That was a sign she was nervous. It was so funny to me that, despite all the years that had passed between us, some things never changed.

"You look good in those glasses," she said instead.

She was deflecting.

"Love? What's going on?"

She sighed. "My dad wants to sell the bar, and I want to save it."

I waved a hand away. "No, I know that. I understand why you want to do that. But when do you think you'll go home? I assume you're only here for a while."

She sighed. "I quit my job."

Oh. Oh Shit.

"Why?" I asked.

She sighed. "Because the CEO of my company was my fiancé."

"And you caught him cheating on you."

She nodded. "Did I mention it was in his office? He was fucking her on his desk during lunch."

I cringed. "Oh, Lila, I'm so sorry."

She shrugged. "Honestly? I'm not. I kept putting off the wedding date. I didn't want to marry him. I didn't love him. Or the last one."

"Last one?"

She sighed, and a pained look came across her face. "It wasn't the first time I was engaged."

Oh.

"You think I'm a terrible person," she said. It was a statement, not a question.

I never thought that about her. I understood why she broke up with me back then. She had been right; long-distance relationships never worked. But nothing else ever worked for me either. Maybe if I got her out of my system, I could let her go. If all she could give me was a couple of weeks, I would take it.

"Declan, I—"

I didn't let her finish that thought. I grabbed her face and kissed her instead. I kissed her in one of her favorite places, trying to show her it didn't matter to me. She slid her hands up my chest, resting them on my polo shirt, but she didn't push me away. She opened to me, letting me slide my tongue inside her mouth. I threaded my hands into her silky brown hair while we pressed our lips together.

I pulled away when I bumped my glasses against her face. "Sorry."

She shook her head with a laugh. "S'okay."

"I don't want to stop kissing you, but I also don't want us to go back to you pretending I don't exist every time you come back into town."

"What are you suggesting?" she asked.

"Let me spend time with you while you're here."

"Declan, I can't give you forever."

I grabbed her hand and kissed the back of her wrist. "Then just give me now."

She nodded, but she still seemed unsure.

I linked my hand with hers. "Come on girl, let's go get you some apple cider donuts."

A smile spread across her face. "They're my favorite."

"I know."

We walked over to the market stall, bought her a donut, and I got myself a coffee. I was beat from how late we had stayed up last night, but it had been worth it. We found Kelsey and her nieces at one of the picnic tables. Kelsey smiled when she saw us.

I sat next to Lila and put my hand on her thigh while she ate her donut and I drank my coffee.

"Aunt Lila, will you help us carve pumpkins?" Cora asked.

Lila smiled. "Of course, sweetie. As long as it's okay with your mommy."

Kelsey nodded and gave us a 'please' look. She looked tired, which made sense if she was in the early stages of her pregnancy. Avery had been like that when she first found out she was pregnant.

"Did you buy a pumpkin yet?" I asked Lila.

She shook her head. "I'm waiting for the right one to call to me." She shivered against the chilly autumn air, and I shrugged out of my jacket and put it over her shoulders.

Kelsey put her head in her hands as she looked at us. "Aw. It's like you two never broke up."

Lila flustered at that. "We're just—"

"Spending time together while Lila's in town," I answered for her.

"Mmmhmm," Kelsey said. "Is that what the kids are calling it these days?"

Lila blushed, and it still looked so cute how her tanned skin reddened in embarrassment. I finished my coffee and took our trash over to the garbage can.

I held my hand out to Lila. "Come on, love, let's go get you a pumpkin."

My girl, who loved fall and Halloween like no one else, broke out into a huge smile. She took my hand, and we walked out onto the field to find her a pumpkin. I knew when she left again, my heart was going to be shattered, but when she smiled at me, I forgot all about that. That was future-Declan's problem.

CHAPTER ELEVEN

LILA

"Watch out, or I'm gonna get you with the pumpkin guts!" Declan teased my niece Cora as we scooped out our pumpkins at my sister's kitchen table.

Cora made a face and pretended to get away from him as he held a scoop of said pumpkin guts into her face. Despite the faces she was making, she loved the attention he was giving her. Kelsey was taking a nap while Callie napped, so we said we'd watch Cora and keep her occupied.

I smiled at how good Declan was with my niece. We tossed the insides of the pumpkins into the trash while Cora decorated her own pumpkin with a glittery face. My sister told me we weren't allowed to let her carve herself, but she could decorate her pumpkin and watch us carve ours. Declan kept her occupied with pumpkin guts and helped her glue on her design while I carved my pumpkin.

I couldn't believe he spent the day with me at the

pumpkin patch with my sister and the kids. He was so good with Cora and didn't mind taking photos of my sister and the kids or holding Callie when she fussed. I won't lie; seeing Callie cuddle into his neck as he talked sweetly to her made me imagine the future we could have had together.

It was a bad idea to start something with him, but the way he was with my nieces made my ovaries melt. And shout at me to let him put a baby in me. I wanted a baby before I was too old, but that ship with Declan sailed long ago. I had to tell my body to be quiet.

"That's very pretty, Cora," I said to my niece as I inspected the jack-o'-lantern face on her pumpkin.

"Auntie Lila?" she asked, her blue eyes inquisitive as she looked up at me.

"What, baby?" I asked, looking up from carving my pumpkin. I threw away the triangle pieces for the eyes I had popped out of the front.

"Are you and Declan gonna have a baby like Mommy and Daddy?"

Declan and I met each other with horrified looks. Where did she get that idea?

Kelsey had been keeping the pregnancy on the down low, but kids were perceptive. Once we got back to my sister's house, Cora asked if she was getting a baby brother or another baby sister. Callie had pointed at Kelsey's stomach and shouted, 'Baby.' So the cat was already out of the bag.

Declan rubbed the back of his neck. "Um."

"No, sweetie," I told her gently. "Declan and I aren't going to have a baby. What made you think that?"

She scrunched her little face up in confusion. "You

were kissing like Mommy and Daddy do. Mommy said when two people love each other, they kiss like that and have a baby."

Declan hid his mouth behind his hand so my niece wouldn't see him laugh. I shot him a glare. "No, sweetie. We're not having a baby."

"Why not?" she asked, and looked mad about it.

I was saved by the front door opening. Cora set down her glitter and jumped out of her chair before we could tell her to wash her hands. "DADDY!" she yelled.

I peered into the living room and saw my brother-in-law holding his daughter in his arms.

A pang of jealousy coursed through me at seeing Brian with his daughter. The clock was ticking on me if I wanted children. I was thinking when I got home, I should look into getting a sperm donor. I wasn't getting any younger and had the money to afford it. The thought of being a single mother by choice didn't appeal to me, though.

Brian walked into the kitchen, and his eyebrows rose in shock at seeing Declan at the table with me. I started working on the nose on my pumpkin, and pretended I didn't see Brian's questioning look.

Brian kissed Cora's head and set her back down in her seat. "What's Auntie Lila got you doing, munchkin?"

"We're making jack-o'-lanterns!" Cora told him excitedly.

I continued to ignore Brian's look as I popped out the nose and threw my pieces in the trash. I started working on the mouth while Declan began on his own jack-o'-lantern face.

"Hey, Declan. Did you actually take a day off at the brewery? I'm shocked!" Brian teased him.

Declan smiled. "Yeah, yeah. Well, ever since Nolan had a baby, he's been on my case about work-life balance."

Brian laughed. "Yeah, man, it's like Avery completely transformed him. He's no longer the biggest Grinch in all of Drakesville."

"Wait, seriously?" I asked.

It was well known that Nolan hated Christmas, which I understood. Their parents had been on their way back from a Christmas party when they were hit by a drunk driver and killed. We had been twelve, and Nolan tried, but Declan knew his heart was never in the holidays after the accident.

"Oh, right, you don't know," Brian said.

"Know what?" I asked, peering at Declan.

"Oh, well, he put up Christmas decorations for Avery, and they got married on Christmas," Declan explained.

I put my carving knife down. "Shut your face! I don't believe it. Your brother?"

Declan pulled out his phone, swiped at it a few times, and then showed me a photo on the brewery's Instagram page. Nolan was in a suit and Avery was wearing a cute vintage-style wedding dress with a flower crown on her head while they stood in front of a Christmas tree. Nolan smiled while he held onto Avery's visibly pregnant belly.

"Wow. Nolan's smiling in that! At Christmas!"

Declan laughed. "Yeah. She brings him out of his grumpy moods."

Brian nudged me. "See? Those are the things you miss when you never come home."

I frowned and couldn't meet either of their eyes.

I heard a commotion from upstairs, and my sister came into the kitchen a few minutes later with Callie on her hip. Brian's face lit up when he saw his wife. He put a hand on her still flat stomach and murmured something to her I couldn't hear. Brian was always so sweet with my sister, and I was glad she got everything she wanted with him.

Declan and I continued to work on our pumpkins in silence. I kept thinking about what my niece asked. There was a time back in high school when I imagined our life together. We'd have the house with a dog and two kids. But I wanted to chase my dreams, so I let him go. And I had been a coward not speaking to him for so long. I could only give him as long as I was in town. This could only be a fling until I went home and sorted my life out.

"Are you two going to stay for dinner?" Kelsey asked.

"I can't," Declan said.

"Oh, right. It's Sunday," Kelsey said.

I eyed Declan in confusion. "What's special about Sunday?"

He sighed. "Avery always makes us have family dinner together."

"Oh."

I popped out the smile on my jack-o'-lantern and threw out the chunks. I cleaned up my work and then held it up for Declan to see. A smile spread across his face, and he held up his own, and I laughed that we both did the same basic design.

"Quit copying me!" I teased and put my pumpkin down.

"It's the only design I can do!"

My sister and her husband were watching us curiously, but I ignored them. Declan and I moved our pumpkins to the counter and then worked at getting rid of the newspaper we had laid on the kitchen table. I wiped down the table while he cleaned up the utensils.

"I better get going," Declan said. "Avery gets mad when anyone's late. The only time I get out of it is if I'm working.

She's already texted me three times that I need to be at dinner tonight."

I smiled. I had liked Avery already, but even more now. She probably saw that Declan and Nolan were workaholics and wanted them to have family time. I admired that about her.

"I better go too. I'm staying with my parents while I'm in town. I have a lot of work to do to find a new website designer."

"Oh. I can do it," Declan offered.

"No, Dec. You've already done the first site."

He rolled his eyes. "Which I did in high school. I made the brewery's site. I can fix it and give you full control."

"Really?"

He nodded.

"I'll pay you," I said firmly.

He shook his head. "Nope."

"Dec, let me give you money. It's going to be a full revamp."

He sighed.

"Oh my God!" my sister cut in. "Stop talking about work and invite her to dinner already!"

Declan grimaced.

Brian laughed. "Get out of here, you two kids."

I rolled my eyes, but we took our pumpkins and walked out of their kitchen.

"Use protection!" Kelsey yelled from the kitchen.

Heat colored my face at her implication, but Declan chuckled beside me as we walked outside to our cars. Then I remembered my car was still at my parents', because Kelsey was going to drive me back after we got home from pumpkin picking. I didn't want to walk over there carrying this pumpkin. It wasn't a long walk, like ten minutes maybe, but carrying something heavy would be a pain in the butt.

Declan put his pumpkin in his car and ran a hand through his hair nervously. "Listen, I—"

"Can you drive me home?"

"Oh, sure," he said, but he frowned and looked disappointed.

"What's wrong?" I asked as I put my pumpkin in the backseat with his and got into the passenger seat.

He went around to the driver's side and started the engine. "Do you want to come for dinner?"

"I don't want to impose."

I was pretty sure Nolan hated my guts, so I didn't want to sit across from him while he glared at me throughout dinner. He told me to stay away from his brother, so he'd probably be pissed if I showed up at his house.

"Avery makes a ton of food, and I want you to come."

"Okay."

He turned to me and gripped my jaw in his big hand. "Then I'm gonna take you home and tie you up again."

I gulped and felt heat pool low in my belly. This Declan was so different from the shy boy I fell in love with at sixteen. Before I could say anything, he slanted his mouth on mine. I melted into his kiss and let him angle my head to get better leverage as he kissed me roughly. He kissed me like a man starved, like kissing me was his way to salvation. I slid my hands behind his neck and let him slip his tongue into my mouth. I let him overtake me in the best way possible.

I was panting and out of breath by the time he pulled away. His glasses were askew, but he fixed them quickly and adjusted himself in his jeans before he pulled his car out of his parking spot.

"I'm sorry," I blurted as we drove to the other side of town.

"For what?" he asked.

"For hurting you."

He sighed. "Love, let's not do this right now."

"But—"

His hand gripped my thigh hard. "Not now, love. Let's go have dinner with my family. Then I can tie you up and punish you for what you did."

I whimpered.

A few minutes later, he pulled into Nolan's driveway and smirked at me when he cut the engine. I checked my makeup in the flip-down mirror. My cheeks were red, and my mouth looked raw from kissing. I found a tube of lipstick in my purse and slid it across my lips. I pursed them together a couple of times, making sure I looked presentable.

Declan looked at me like he was the big, bad wolf about to eat me up.

"What?" I asked and put my lipstick away.

"Can't wait to watch that smear across my dick while I fuck your face later."

"DECLAN!" I scolded.

He gave me a devilish grin. "What? You know you'll love it."

"Dirty, dirty man," I teased.

He kissed my neck. "You love it, naughty girl."

"Stop! I can't go into your brother's house with wet panties."

"That sounds like a 'you' problem," he teased, then he got out of the car.

Dick.

I pressed my thighs together and tried to calm down.

This man was so dirty and dominating; I couldn't wait to be at his mercy again later. I didn't care if this was just going to be a fling. I was going to love every single minute of being with him.

I got out of the car and followed him inside the house. We walked into the kitchen and found Avery and Nolan at the kitchen counter, working on dinner together. At the table was an older man with a shock of white hair holding baby Norah. Next to him were Gemma and the tattooed bartender, but there was also a teenage girl with dark hair.

Avery turned around at the sound of our footsteps in the kitchen. "Look who it is!" Avery said, then she noticed me. "Oh, hi, Lila! Nice to see you too."

"I hope you don't mind me imposing," I said. "Declan invited me last minute. Do you need help with anything?"

Avery waved her hand at me. "Not at all. Sit down. Nolan and I got this."

Nolan ignored me, which I guessed was better than him glaring at me. I sat in the empty chair next to Gemma while Declan went into the fridge and got us beers. He sat down next to me and handed me a beer.

"Oh, I love this beer," I said as I drank the pumpkin beer down.

Declan smiled as he sipped on a Drakesville Lager.

"Oh, you met my boyfriend Felix at the brewery," Gemma said, introducing her boyfriend, and then she pointed to the teenager. "And his sister Skye. This is my dad."

I waved to them.

Gemma's dad peered at me for a second. "You're Kelly and Sean's daughter, right?"

I nodded.

"I heard they're selling the bar. That's a shame."

"Not if I can help it!" I exclaimed.

Gemma got an excited look in her eye. "Oh, so the Irish food at the Harvest Fest was amazing. Felix is working on redesigning the menu."

I furrowed my brow at her.

Felix shrugged. "Brian and I got to talking when we were manning the table together."

"Did he pay you? Because I want to make sure all of you get paid for your time and energy. I want the bar to succeed."

Felix shook his head. "I sent him an invoice for a deposit, but he said you were the capital."

"Good." I turned to Declan. "I'm serious about earlier. Send me an invoice when you're done with the website."

"What website?" Nolan asked when he and Avery walked over to the table, bringing dinner over for everyone.

Declan put his hand on my thigh. "I'm going to help redesign Sullivan's website."

"Oh, good!" Gemma cheered. "Oh, I have some PR people that might help, too. I'll email them to you."

"Gemma, that's amazing," I said.

"Okay, no work chat, time to eat!" Avery exclaimed, and we all shut up.

We started with the salad and then moved on to the delicious chicken parmesan main course. Avery was an amazing cook. I was decent in the kitchen, but it was hard working so many hours that I ended up eating a lot of take-out.

"So, how long are you in town for?" Avery asked.

I shrugged. "Not sure yet. To be honest, I came back to save the bar."

"But your dad still wants to sell?" Nolan asked. He ate one-handed while he held Norah in his other hand.

Avery tried to take her off him a while ago, but he wanted her to eat first. It was cute how much he worshiped his wife.

"I have to convince him not to," I explained.

"Where in California do you live?" Gemma asked.

"Silicon Valley. It's nice, but I'm glad I came in now. I love this time of year."

Nolan eyed his brother. "Well, if you got him to take a day off, I'm glad."

He didn't seem so glad when he talked to me last time. But I noticed the warning glare Declan sent him when Nolan sat down.

"Well," Avery said. "We're glad you could join us for dinner. Declan never brings a guest."

Nolan grumbled something under his breath.

"Spit it out," Declan spat at him.

Nolan shook his head.

"No. Say what you have to say," Declan insisted.

Nolan sighed. "I'm just wondering how long it will take until I have to pick up your pieces again when she leaves and breaks your heart."

Gemma got wide-eyed, and Felix looked down at his plate, pretending not to witness Nolan's outburst. Skye looked like she wanted all the tea. This was exactly why I hadn't wanted to come to dinner.

"I'm a grown-ass man. You don't get to say shit about who I spend my time with," Declan snarled.

I put a hand on Declan's arm. "No, it's okay. Nolan's right. Nol, I know you're trying to protect your brother, but I'm not trying to hurt him."

Nolan gestured between the two of us. "So, what is all this?"

"It's not any of your business," Declan seethed.

"We're spending time together. Declan was my best friend for several years, that's all," I said.

Norah started crying, which diffused the situation.

But I knew he was right. Nolan was right to ask why I showed up for family dinner. Right to ask what I thought I was doing with his brother. I wished I had an answer for him because I didn't know either.

CHAPTER TWELVE

DECLAN

Lila lay naked and spent in my arms after I had her spread eagle across my bed and made her beg for it. She was so hot when she whimpered and cried out for my dick before I gave it to her hard and rough.

"What's wrong, love?" I asked and kissed her hair.

She shook her head.

She had been quiet since we left my brother's place, and it was no surprise why. I was going to have words with Nolan later. He had no right to be downright rude to her face like that. It embarrassed Avery, so I was sure she would give him a piece of her mind too.

"I should go," she whispered into my chest, but didn't make a move to get out of my arms.

"Hey, tell me what's wrong."

She sighed. "Nol's right. I'm going to hurt you again."

I shook my head and tilted her head up to look at me. "I'm a big boy."

"But Dec—"

I silenced her by putting a finger on her lips. "Okay, how about we just enjoy what this is?"

"What do you mean?"

I gestured between the two of us. "We spend time with each other, in my bed and out, while you're here, and when you go home, that's the end."

"Like a fling?" she asked.

"Sure, if you want. But when you go home, we'll still be friends. You won't pretend I don't exist when you come home for the holidays."

She chewed on her lip as she thought about it. "Why do you want that?"

I twirled a strand of her hair around my finger. "Because I missed you."

A smile tugged at the corner of her lips. "I missed you too. I missed you so much, but I didn't want to see you again because I was afraid I wouldn't finish my degree."

"I know, love. I know why you broke up with me back then, and that's okay."

"Did you hate me?" she asked.

No. I never hated her. Could never, ever hate her. She broke my heart, but I never had a single hateful bone in my body for her. I loved her far too much for that.

I shook my head and kissed the back of her wrist. "No, my love. I could never hate you."

"Really?" she asked, her eyes welling up with tears.

I cupped her face. "What's with the tears?"

She wiped her eyes. "I know how much I hurt you."

"I know, love, but we were teenagers. Things are different now."

She nodded. "Okay. I had fun with you today. It was like old times. Except..." she blushed. "Except when you tied me to the bed, that was different."

I sat up and shifted her into my lap. She curled into me as I cradled her in my arms. "But you liked that, right?"

She nodded. "I'll tell you if I don't. It's so sexy how dominating you are."

I nuzzled into her neck and kissed her. "Good. Now stay."

She laughed and pushed me away. She got out of bed and started looking around for her clothes. "I can't. My mom has been blowing up my phone, asking where I am. I'm thirty-four, and she has to keep tabs on me."

I laid back on the bed and put my hands behind my head. "Tell her you're with me."

She shook her head as she pulled on her jeans. "I have work to do tomorrow."

"Like what?" I asked.

She pulled on her bra, but I wanted her to take it off and crawl back into bed with me. "I need to find someone to do our marketing. Brian's trying with the social media, but I don't think he's good at it. You sure I can't steal Gemma?"

"Fuck no! I had to fight to keep her."

She cocked her head at me.

"Gemma didn't want the job at first. I had to force her on vacation and then..."

"Then what?"

I smirked. "Avery and I meddled."

"Explain yourself!"

"Get your fine ass back in bed and I will."

She looked like she was thinking about it for a moment, then she took her jeans off and crawled back into the bed with me. She slid in next to me, and I put my arm around her.

"Felix needed a vacation badly, so I gave him and Gemma time off at the same time. Avery told Felix he could stay at her dad's cabin in the Poconos, and then I convinced her to tell Gemma to go there for her forced vacation, too."

"Why?"

I put my glasses back on so I could see her when I looked at her. "Because they bickered too much, and it was annoying to work with. But then they had a huge misunderstanding when they got back, and Gemma quit the brewery."

Lila gasped. "What? She loves the brewery!"

I nodded. "Felix had to do a lot of groveling, but they're good now."

She laid her head on my shoulder. "Aw, you're a little matchmaker. Do they know you and Avery colluded together?"

"Nope, and you better not tell anyone."

She grinned and looked up at me. "What will happen if I do?"

"You know what happens if you break the rules, naughty girl," I said and bent to kiss her again.

"I'm not going home tonight, am I?"

I shook my head. "Not if I can help it."

She leaped up to get her phone on the bedside table. "I have to text my mom, or she'll think I'm dead."

I laughed. "Okay, love."

I watched her type away on her phone, and I wanted to freeze this moment of her in her underwear on my bed with that sweet smile on her face. I wanted to memorize this moment because even though I suggested this fling, I knew as soon as she left, I'd feel like a shell of a man again. I wanted to remind myself later how good it felt when she was in my arms.

She gave me an annoyed look. "Why are you creeping on me?"

I brushed her hair behind her ear and bent to take her mouth again, this time slow and lingering. I kissed her until we were tangled up in my sheets, until I was unhooking her bra and sliding her panties down her legs. I kissed her through all her orgasms as we had slow, gentle sex.

Sometimes having vanilla sex was nice. I didn't always need to have her tied up and submissive to me. I just needed to be with her. Needed to feel myself pressed so deep inside her, worshiping her body like the goddess she was.

I was in deep trouble already. Seeing Lila again was like nothing had ever happened. We bounced back as if sixteen years weren't between us. Like we were still those kids who had hopes of being together forever. I pretended that was who we still were. Pretended like it wasn't going to hurt when she walked out of my life again.

※

Lila was still asleep when I woke up the next morning. I slipped out of bed and went into my tiny kitchen to make us coffee. The brewery didn't open until noon, and I usually didn't go in until then. So why was I up at eight in the morning? To work on the website for her.

I sat down at my table in my kitchen and opened my computer. I scanned the website for Sullivan's Bar and groaned at how outdated it was. I designed this back in high school as part of my computer science elective. Over the years, I had offered to redesign it for Lila's parents, but they always said it was fine. It was a hot mess and needed a total overhaul.

A part of me wondered if I should fix it at all. The longer she stayed in Drakesville, the longer I'd get to spend time with her. If I fixed this quickly, then she'd leave me sooner. But that was a total dick move.

I grabbed a cup of coffee and got to work, pushing aside my selfish thoughts. I clicked another tab to look at the brewery's website and opened some other bar websites to get inspiration, but then I searched Lila's name instead.

The first thing that popped up was a photo of her at a Gala with some nerdy-looking guy with glasses on her arm. Dark hair, plastic rim glasses, a skinny guy with no muscles, yeah, it was safe to say Lila had a type. He wore a suit, and she was dressed impeccably in a sparkling slinky black evening gown. She was like the brightest star in the sky next to him.

I read the caption on the photo. *Chad Banks, CEO of Hedy Industries, with fiancée Lila Sullivan.*

I looked up Hedy Industries and scoffed at the reason for calling it that. Seriously? Because the guy had a hard-on for Hedy Lamarr? What a douche canoe. I found Lila's LinkedIn when I went back to my search engine. There was a headshot, and it listed her as 'inside counsel for Hedy Industries.' I didn't know what exactly she did, but her parents proudly told me she was raking in the big bucks as a lawyer for some tech firm. Why would she want to throw it all away for some bar in the Philly suburbs?

I looked around my claustrophobic apartment. There wasn't much to my place, but I had lived here for the past couple of years because it was close to the brewery. Lila was probably used to fancy cars and mansion-style houses, nothing like my tiny apartment.

I closed out those tabs and tried to get back to work. But my mind kept returning to the fact that I was so far beneath her. Owning a brewery meant you were always worried about the bottom line. Always worried a bad batch could set you back. Nolan and I had been making a name for ourselves. We were living comfortably, but not in the luxury like Lila was. What did she even want to do with me, anyway?

I tried to shake those thoughts away as I sipped my coffee and started working on a new design. I wanted to lean into the Irish stuff since that's what Gemma suggested. Maybe they needed a new logo too.

I shot off a text to Felix.

ME: *Can you do a logo concept for me?*

Felix was up early because he was getting his little sister, Skye, off to school this morning. I wasn't surprised when he texted me right back.

FELIX: *For your girlfriend's bar?*

ME: *Ex-girlfriend.*

FELIX: *Who you're totally banging tho, right?*

ME: *Shut it. Can you do it or not?*

FELIX: *Yeah man, I got it.*

I got lost in the code as I figured out what I wanted from this new website. It had to have a clean design, but we needed to get more assets to make this work. The stuff currently on the website was so old.

I jumped when I felt a hand wrap around my bare chest, but a smile painted across my face when I looked up at Lila.

"Sorry, you looked like you were in the zone," she said. She pressed a kiss to my neck and looked at my computer screen. "How long have you been awake?"

I checked my phone and realized I had been at it for two hours. I let her sleep in until ten. "Sorry, a while. We have some problems."

She slid into my lap and wrapped her arms around the back of my neck. She was wearing one of my t-shirts, and something animalistic crawled up inside and beat at my chest because it made it seem like she was mine. I gave her a long, lingering kiss good morning. She pressed her forehead against mine and cupped my face gently as we kissed.

"My love?" I asked when I reluctantly pulled away.

"Hmm?"

"You better stop that."

She gave me a naughty grin. "Or what?"

Oh, she was such a brat, and I loved it. Loved that she pretended to struggle when I had her in the restraints. Or she pretended to be bad because she wanted her punishment. I never imagined she would have the same kinks as me.

I slid the t-shirt up her long legs and pulled her down against my morning wood. "Feel what you do to me."

She arched her back and ground onto my dick. "Mmm, love that."

"Focus, it's not playtime."

She pouted. "But I want to play."

"Not now. We gotta talk business."

She was still pouting.

Such a brat. I wanted nothing more than to knock all the stuff off my kitchen table and bend her over it, fucking her until she screamed my name. But I had to control my urges. I had to be the adult right now.

"I asked Felix to whip up a new logo," I said.

"You did?" she asked, her eyes lighting up in surprise. "I'll pay him. You don't pay for it."

"Okay, okay. I'll ask him to invoice you. We need new photos, better photos. Who's doing your social media?"

She frowned. "Brian? It's not great."

I rubbed my jaw as I thought. "You might need to hire a marketing specialist."

She nodded in agreement. "I already want to do that. That's why I wanted to go home last night, but someone wanted me all to himself."

"Can't help it. I want to have you as much as I can until you go back to your real life."

She frowned, but I kissed her so she couldn't argue with me. Then I took her back to my bed.

CHAPTER THIRTEEN

LILA

My parents were already at the bar when Declan drove me home. He only did that because he didn't want me to walk with my huge pumpkin. I hadn't tried to protest, mostly because my brain was in a fog from all the sex we had last night and then again this morning. We had slow vanilla sex the last two times, and I liked that as much as the rough stuff. But it felt like he was making love to me in those moments, making me wonder if a fling with him was a good idea.

I showered when I got home and moaned in pain when I realized how sore my thighs were. Declan MacGregor was going to wear me out.

I got dressed and walked over to the bar. I hadn't expected to wake up and find Declan already working on the new website, but he gave me some things to think about.

I went into the office and found my dad looking frantic. I put my computer bag down next to the desk. "What's wrong?" I asked.

He ran a hand through his white hair. "Sarah called out sick. We're going to hit a lunch rush soon, and I'm short a server."

It only took me a second to think of a solution. "I can help."

"Sweetheart, no."

"Dad, that's why I came here, to help the bar in any way I can. You got any extra Sullivan's shirts?"

Good thing I had worn black jeans today, not that Dad would care if I wasn't wearing the standard dress pants that were the server uniforms. Thank god my parents didn't go for that short plaid skirt thing a lot of Irish bars did. Someone suggested that one time and Dad got heated and said, 'We're not the Tilted Kilt!'

Dad got up and went into the closet. He pulled out an old black polo shirt with the Sullivan's Bar lettering on the front. Declan was right to ask Felix to come up with a new logo. Ours was just lettering with our name and nothing more. It was so boring.

Dad looked stressed, but I went into the bathroom and got changed. When I came back into the office, I got an idea. "Dad, take a photo of me in uniform at the bar."

"Why?"

"Just do it. I have an idea."

We walked out to the front, and I got behind the bar. My mom was wiping down the bar, and her smile went ear-to-ear when she saw me. "Oh, it's just like old times!"

I pretended to pour a beer from one of the taps while Dad took my photo with my phone. I stopped what I was doing and took my phone back from him. "Mom, do you have the login info for the Instagram account?"

"It's in the office."

I rolled my eyes. Yes, let's leave our password info out in the open. Because that is so smart!

I went into the office and found the sticky note on the computer. I logged into the account and posted the photo with a caption that read, *It's not Throwback Thursday, but this Monday, get a blast from the past as our very own Lila Sullivan will be serving you at Sullivan's bar. Come get a pint with us today and sample our new traditional Irish specials. #SullivansBar #Drakesville #DrinkLocal #IrishBar*

I put my phone back in my pocket and went out onto the floor. We had just opened, and only a few customers had trickled in so far, but the late lunch crowd would start to come in. I went over to the chalkboard and started writing the new specials. If we started putting the Shepard's pie and potato pasties onto the specials board, it wouldn't be a shock when we released the new menu.

Brian was behind the bar with his brother, Killian, one of our bartenders. I went to the seating chart to check which section Sarah was supposed to be in, and found that none of my tables were seated yet.

"Do you even remember how to wait tables?" Killian asked when I sat at the bar and rolled silverware.

I glared at him. "I've been working in this place a lot longer than you."

He crossed his big arms over his chest. "Yeah, but aren't you like a hotshot lawyer now?"

"Sure. But I still know how to wait tables."

Brian nudged his younger brother. "Ignore him. He's an asshole."

"Oh, I'm aware. He used to pull my hair in the fourth grade," I said.

"You liked it," Killian teased.

I felt my face get hot because I *did* like that, but I didn't want them to know that.

Luckily, a few more parties came into the bar, so I didn't have to entertain the Murphy Brothers anymore. The bar got busy as I rushed around waiting tables. I messed up a few things, but waiting tables was like riding a bike. As soon as I got used to it, it was like second nature. Like I had been born for it. In some ways, I guessed I had been.

By the time we had another lull in customers, I was bussing all the tables and making sure everyone was cashed out. Mom told me to take a break, but I ended up shoving a grilled cheese into my face while I monitored our social media. There were a lot of comments on the post I put up this morning.

I saw we were tagged in something from the brewery's profile. I clicked on it and saw an image of Nolan and one of the other brewers hard at work in the tank room. The comment read, *We're partnering up with Sullivan's Bar to bring you an exclusive new beer. ONLY available at Sullivan's Bar and the MacGregor Brothers Brewing Company Brew Pub. More details soon. #MacGregorBrothersBrewingCompany #SullivansBar #Drakesville #DrinkLocal #PABeer*

There were a lot of comments on that post. Gemma was great at this stuff. I wished I could be as good at it as she was. I still didn't know how long I'd be in town helping my parents. The beer would take a while, but I wanted to make sure my dad didn't sell by the time I left. I also wanted to make sure Declan finished the website.

That reminded me of something.

I threw away my trash and went out into the front to find Brian. He was talking to one of the locals at the bar, but Killian was standing there pretending to clean. My mom was back in the kitchen while Dad was in the office doing inventory.

"Lila Sullivan, I can't believe that's you!" the customer talking to Brian exclaimed. I realized he was my high school history teacher, Mr. Davies. He had a soft spot for me.

"Hi, Mr. Davies, how are you?"

"Good. Enjoying retirement."

"Good for you."

"What are you doing waiting tables? Your dad said you're a big shot lawyer now."

There was that phrase again. I made a lot of money, and some people knew who I was because of Chad, but big shot, I wasn't so sure.

I shrugged. "Just helping out the bar for a little bit."

He pointed at me. "You tell that dad of yours not to sell."

"That's what I'm trying to do!" I told him with a smile.

Brian cashed Mr. Davies out, and I waved goodbye to him. I waited for Brian to pay attention to me. "What?" he asked.

"Do we know any good photographers?"

"Why?"

"Declan's working on the website, and our photos are oolllld."

"Lachlan," Killian said. "We can get him to do it for free."

Brian grinned. "We can bully him into it."

Lachlan was their youngest brother. He was the quietest of the Murphy bunch. I always felt sorry for him since they bullied him so much. That was the curse of being the baby in a big family. Or his brothers were just a bunch of dicks. Both were probably true.

I waved them off. "Doesn't matter. I'll pay him. Felix is

going to do a new logo for us too. Gemma thinks we need to lean into the Irish stuff."

"Is that why we have Shepard's pie as a special today?" Killian asked and made a face.

I nodded. "You have a problem with traditional food? Where's your heritage?"

Killian stuck out his tongue at me. "Yeah, it's fucking gross."

"I'll talk to him," Brian said to me, ignoring his brother.

I nodded. "Okay, good. I'm thinking we need a photo of Mom and Pops, our food, and the bar. I'll ask Declan if he's looking for something specific."

"Mmmhmm," Brian said and gave me a look.

I nudged him. "What gives?"

"Heard you didn't come home the last two nights."

"Oohhh," Killian teased.

"You guys are dicks. It's none of your business," I snapped.

I forgot how living in a small town could be such an enormous pain in my ass. Because your family could be all up in your business all the time. Especially mine. When my sister married Brian Murphy, I forgot he came with four annoying younger brothers.

Brian cashed me out, and luckily for me, happy hour started, so Killian got busy. I was glad about that because I couldn't deal with either of them getting on my case about Declan. I truly didn't know how long it would take to get my parents back on their feet, but I'd be here as long as they needed me. Not like I had a job to get back to.

I took off my apron and went into the office. My dad was at the desk punching in some numbers.

"Dad."

He turned to me. "Hey, sweetheart. Thanks for helping. You didn't need to."

I handed him a wad of cash from my tips. "Here."

He waved me away. "Keep it. You earned that."

I tucked it back into my purse, but I was going to stick it in the safe later. "Okay, can we talk numbers now?"

He shook his head. "That's not your problem."

"Dad, let me help."

He raised an eyebrow at me. "Where have you been the past couple of nights?"

I reared back at his abrupt change in the conversation. Where had that come from?

"What does that have to do with anything?"

He eyed me suspiciously. "Your sister said Declan MacGregor went pumpkin picking with you yesterday, and you went home with him."

I clenched my jaw tightly. Tattle-tell. "Okay. What does that have to do with the bar?"

"Because he asked me for assets today because he's redoing the website."

I sighed. "We're spending time together, and he wants to help. I'm paying him for the work. Actually, Brian's going to talk to his younger brother to get some new photos done for it."

"Lachlan?" Dad asked.

I nodded. "I didn't realize he was into photography."

"That's because you haven't lived here in a long time."

Ouch, but fair.

"What does it matter if I spend time with Declan?" I asked.

Dad gave me a stern look. "Because last time you left, he lost himself."

I wasn't sure how to tell my dad I had also lost myself. I

chased my dreams in college, but I never found happiness. I wasn't saying that Declan and I had a future together, but I enjoyed spending time with him.

"That's not gonna happen this time. I'm not going to pretend he doesn't exist when I leave," I explained.

Dad snorted, and I immediately got annoyed with him. What right did he have to butt into my sex life? NONE. That's what right he had.

"I'm gonna go home," I said.

I left without another word and walked home annoyed. The fact my dad cared more about Declan's feelings than mine bothered me. Everyone seemed so concerned with how he felt after I left, but nobody asked if leaving him hurt me too.

I ate leftovers in front of the TV, watching a Bulldogs hockey game while my parents were still at the bar. I missed watching my home team. I only agreed to marry Chad because he proposed during a San Jose hockey game. On the jumbotron. Public proposals were the worst. Later he said he did it because he thought I loved hockey. He didn't get that I was a Philly girl through and through. It was Bulldogs, Phils, Eagles, Sixers, and nothing else. I didn't give a crap about the local hockey team.

The door opened and distracted me from the game. I waved at my mom as she walked inside. "Hey, sweetheart. Is that your pumpkin on the porch?"

I nodded. "Yeah, we carved pumpkins yesterday. I forgot how much I missed fall in PA. Nobody wants to do that stuff with me out West."

She smiled as she took a seat next to me. "Thanks for picking up the shift today."

I shrugged her off. "That's why I came home, to help you out. Whatever you need."

She nudged me with a smile on her face. "That post on our social media did really well. Good job."

"We need to find someone to do that. I think I want to find a marketing person to help us out."

Mom hugged me. "I'm glad you're home. You're not with Declan tonight?"

Mom's eyes sparkled with mirth. She had been holding out for me and Declan to get back together forever, and she had called me a coward more than once about avoiding him. My parents loved Declan and hated everyone I dated after him.

I shrugged. "We didn't make plans. Mom, we're not getting back together."

"But you said you still have feelings for him!"

I sighed. "Mom, I'm not moving home."

She raised a dark eyebrow at me. "Yet you slept at his place the last couple of nights."

"Mom, I'm an adult!"

"Okay..."

I rolled my eyes. "Goodbye, MOTHER! I'm getting a shower and going to bed."

When I got out of the shower, I saw a text message from Declan. A sexy text message. He sent me a shirtless photo of him lying in his bed wearing his glasses. A second text came through from him.

DECLAN: *My bed's so lonely without you tonight.*

I smirked at the fact he was sending me thirst traps. He looked so hot in those glasses. I might have a thing for nerdy guys. I was glad he remembered to ask for my phone number before I left this morning.

ME: *I'm soooo tired. Did a shift at the bar today.*

DECLAN: [*Pleading face emoji*]

ME: *STOP! I'm sooo tired, babe. You kept me up so late.*

DECLAN: *I sleep better with you in my arms.*

My heart was doing cartwheels in my chest at his words. I was giddy like a teenager wanting to sneak out to meet her boyfriend. Not a thirty-four-year-old woman about to have another booty call with her ex-boyfriend.

I got dressed, packed a small bag with a change of clothes, and walked down the stairs. Mom looked up at the sound of my footsteps and gave me a knowing grin. "Tell Declan we said hello."

"Bye!" I called after her, ignoring her comment.

This might be a bad idea, spending all my waking moments with him, but when I was in his arms, when he kissed me, it was like time stood still. Like all these years hadn't passed. Like we were meant for each other. And I didn't want that feeling to stop.

CHAPTER FOURTEEN

DECLAN

I pushed my glasses up on my head and rubbed the sleep from my eyes. Nolan made a comment about how I had been better at my work-life balance this past week, but he didn't know I wasn't working twelve-hour days at the brewery because, in my spare time, I was working on the website redesign for the Sullivans. And when I wasn't doing that, I spent as much time as possible with Lila.

I rubbed a hand across Lila's thigh as she sat up in my bed beside me, working on her own spreadsheets. This past week she'd been picking up shifts at her parents' bar since one of their wait staff had quit on the spot. She had also hired a marketing firm to help them get out of the red. She worked a double tonight, so when she came over, we hopped into the shower together and had acrobatic sex in there.

"How's the beer coming along?" she asked me without looking up at whatever she was reading on her computer.

I shrugged. "That's Nolan's gig, but he seems happy so far."

"Dad's excited about it."

I squeezed her thigh and worked on coding while she scrolled on her computer.

"Did the photos turn out okay?" she asked.

I nodded. "Yeah. They're great."

She closed the lid of her laptop but didn't ask me to stop working. I felt her staring at me, and when I turned to her, she had that bright smile painted across her face. I loved that her smile radiated across her whole body. Like it was only for me.

"What?" I asked.

"I love when you wear your glasses," she said, reaching a hand up to stroke my face. "So sexy."

"Yeah, you got a thing for nerds, huh?"

"Maybe..." she trailed off, and then tried to get a peek at the website.

I shifted away from her. "Nope, you only get to see it when I'm done."

She pouted. "Please, Dec. I want to see the progress."

"Well, you need to answer about the logo first."

She frowned. "Dad can't decide! Felix did an amazing job."

"Let's look at them again," I suggested.

I pulled up Felix's designs on my computer, and we looked at them together. Lila stared at my screen and wrinkled her nose as she thought about it.

Felix gave us three logo concepts. One was a circular logo with a brown background and a green four-leaf clover in the center. Above the clover, read 'SULLIVAN'S' across the top, and then down below it read 'BAR.' The second one was another circular logo with a Celtic knot design as a border. The rest of the circle was blocked out in green with a harp in the center. The word 'SULLIVAN'S' was written around the top above the harp, and then 'IRISH PUB' was below it. The third one was rectangular with a brown background and had green four-leaf clovers on each corner. In the center was a pint of beer, with 'SULLIVAN'S' above the pint glass and 'BAR' below it.

I pulled up his notes again to reread them.

Hey,

Here are three concepts. Any of them can be changed to have it as Sullivan's Bar or Sullivan's Irish Pub. I know the name has been Sullivan's Bar forever, but Gemma suggested a rebrand to compete with other Irish pubs and to have a similar look people think of. I think it will fit the aesthetic, especially with the new menu.

"What's your favorite?" I asked her.

She chewed on her lip. "I think Gemma's right about calling it an Irish Pub, but I'm afraid that since we've been called a bar for so long, it will confuse people."

"Okay, not my question. If you had to choose, which would it be?"

She peered at my computer again for a couple of seconds. "The harp one. My mom and Kelsey like that one too, but Dad's the owner, so I need him to decide."

"That's my favorite too, and yeah, I agree with Gemma, too. Call it a pub. All the other Irish bars are called pubs. It fits in with the branding. As soon as we make a decision, Felix can start incorporating it into the menu redesign."

She grimaced. "Good, because I'm pretty sure we're printing it out on computer paper right now. But maybe if you like that one too, that gives me extra firepower."

"Why's that?"

She rolled her eyes. "Because my dad loves you, and your opinion probably means more than mine."

I frowned. "That's not true."

"Yeah, it is."

I closed my laptop and got up to put it on my desk. I glared at Lila when I noticed her dirty towel and clothes strewn about on my floor. I picked those up and aggressively threw them in my hamper.

She laughed. "You're so anal, Dec!"

"I like things in their proper place."

"Such a control freak."

I crawled back into the bed with her and pulled her against my chest. "You seem to like it when I'm in control."

Heat colored her face, but that didn't stop her from grinning at me. "Maybe..."

I gripped her jaw. "Yeah, you do."

She nodded. "I do."

"There's my good girl," I purred.

I didn't care that it was already late; I didn't have to open the brewery until noon, anyway. Lila didn't seem to care either, as we spent the next hour making each other come as much as possible.

I knew all this had a time stamp. Eventually, she'd go back to California, but I didn't care about any of that when she was in my arms.

🍁

"Look at you strolling in late," Gemma teased when I walked into the office way later than I intended to the next day.

"Shut it, Gem," I said as I took my seat behind my desk.

She eyed me suspiciously. "You've been acting weird lately."

If by weird, she meant happy, that was mostly because I was getting laid on the regular. That was all because of Lila. I told my heart to simmer down because this was all about my dick, but that didn't stop me from smiling when she was with me. Or being in a good mood because I got to have her in my arms every night.

"You and Nol have way more in common than I realized," she said.

"How so?" I asked.

I turned on my computer and opened up my sales report for the week. I had to admit, the pumpkin beer was selling well. It was October, though, so we couldn't bank completely on the seasonal beers to carry us through. I had a meeting with the sales team later to go over projections and make sure we were on target with our goals.

"Because you're both weak for your women!" Gemma teased.

I scoffed at her. "She's not my woman."

Gemma pinned me with an annoyed stare. "That's bullshit, and you know it. Since Lila came back to town, you've been a completely different person."

"Are you ever gonna stop being a pain in my ass?"

Gemma grinned from ear to ear like the annoying little sister she was. "You know I'm right!"

"Butt out of it, Gem."

She glared at me. "Oh no! You don't give me that. You're a meddlesome fucker. Avery told me you were the one who told her to convince me to go to the cabin last summer and forced me to deal with Felix."

I grinned. "Worked, didn't it?"

"Not the point!"

"Get to work, Gem. Get off my dick."

"Someone's been on your dick a lot," she muttered.

"None of your business."

"Just...be careful."

I was getting tired of people telling me to be careful, as if I wasn't a grown adult who could make his own decisions.

Gemma turned around and went back to her work while I did my own. She got the hint that I didn't want to talk about it anymore. She was hard at work organizing the Halloween party in a couple of weeks, so she was busy enough that she didn't have time to bother me.

I buried myself in work for the rest of the day and was still in the middle of it when Gemma left for the day. Nolan came in a few hours ago to check in with me, but he was working on brewing the new beer and hadn't bothered me since.

I was eating dinner at my desk as I finished payroll for the week when my phone vibrated. A smile spread across my face when Lila's name popped up on my screen. I hadn't heard from her all day, but I knew she was busy helping interview a new server and meeting with her marketing consultant today.

My eyes widened at the photo on my screen. Lila was lying in my bed in black see-through lingerie. A naughty smile played across her lips, and her dark hair fanned out on the pillow like she was an angel. A sexy angel ready and waiting for me.

I gulped and felt my dick thicken against my leg. I read the accompanying text.

LILA: *Come play with me!*

ME: *Love, you're killing me.*

I squeezed my eyes shut when she sent another photo of her hands down those see-through panties. Fuck me. I could finish this later. I saved my work and shut down my computer for the night. I nearly ran out of the brewery and over to my apartment a couple of doors down. Thank god I lived so close.

I had given Lila a spare key yesterday after she came in late from closing down the bar. I didn't regret that at all if she was lying in my bed in sexy lingerie waiting for me. My dick was enraged against my leg, and I wanted to get upstairs as quickly as possible to pound into her perfect pussy.

I kicked off my shoes and walked into the bedroom. Lila lay on the bed with her eyes closed and her back arched as she fingered herself. She looked sexy as hell touching herself in my bed, but *I* was supposed to make her come. That should be my hands or cock or tongue, making her moan.

She yelped in surprise when I crawled on top of her and pressed her hands above her head. Her hazel eyes were wide with excitement as I bent over her. "Naughty girl," I growled.

"You were taking too long," she said and rocked against my hands.

I wagged my finger at her. "No, my love, you know the rules."

"Please, baby?" she begged.

I couldn't take it anymore. If I wasn't inside her at this exact moment, I was going to explode. I kept her hands above her head with one hand, and with the other, I undid my jeans and released my dick from my boxers. Without thinking, I pushed her panties to the side and plunged my dick inside. I needed to be inside her so badly. I didn't even think about lube, and I always used that.

She wrapped her legs around my waist, and I noticed she wore black stockings clipped to her lingerie with black fuck-me heels on her feet. This woman knew exactly what I wanted at all times, and I loved that about her.

I held her hands down against the bed while I thrust all the way home. I wasn't thinking about protection. I just needed to be buried deep inside her. She met my every urgent thrust with an arch of her hips and a cry of pleasure.

"More," she begged as we rocked together fast and urgent, as if we were racing to the finish line of our orgasms together.

I slid out slowly and then slammed back in, groaning at the sound of her cries as she moaned my name repeatedly. She rocked against my grip on her hands and tried to get away from my grasp. But it was all a game. She loved being at my mercy and being held down while I fucked her into oblivion. She liked that I made her come undone when I stroked inside her so deep that she forgot her name.

"Baby," she moaned.

I locked our fingers together, holding her down and fucking her through her orgasm. She panted beneath me and arched up against me so we could become one again. The headboard slapped against the wall with each thrust as I took her over the edge, over and over again.

"Come inside me," she begged. "I want it, please."

She dug her heels into my back while I stroked harder. The bed smacked against the wall, echoing the sounds of our bodies slamming together. I squeezed my eyes shut as I slid in and out, harder and faster, pressing her down into the mattress until I came in long spurts inside her.

It took me a moment to catch my breath. My chest

heaved heavily as I came down from the intense orgasm. I hadn't been gentle. I had been rough and wild with her, like the beast she brought out in me. I unlinked our hands and pressed small kisses on her wrists like I always did after restraining her.

She cupped my face and pulled me down for a slow kiss. I reluctantly pulled away when I felt myself get soft inside her. I pulled out and looked down in horror when I realized we didn't use a condom. I *never* did that. I wanted kids, but on my own terms, with someone who loved me, not with my high school sweetheart, who was only a temporary fix.

"Baby, what's wrong?" she asked, her eyes full of concern. She cradled my face in her hands as we looked into each other's eyes.

I gestured to my dick. "Shit, Lila, I forgot to wrap it up!"

She looked down between her legs. I was still in-between them, and my cum dripped down and spilled all over her panties. I had painted her with my cum in my desperate need to make her mine.

"Oh...that's okay. I'm on the pill," she said.

I put her underwear back in place. I hadn't even taken her lingerie off yet. I was such a horny asshole I fucked her with her underwear still on.

She pulled me back down to her for another rough kiss, surprising me when she suddenly pushed me onto my back and climbed on top of me. She pressed her hands on my chest. "It was so hot, baby. You were like a wild animal coming in here all hot and bothered that you couldn't wait to get that big dick inside me. You just had to have me."

I reached a hand around and slapped her ass. Her cheeks were bare in the tiny thong she wore, and surprisingly my dick was getting hard again already. "So naughty, I couldn't help myself."

She bounced on my lap. "It was so hot when you filled me up bare. I felt every last inch of your amazing cock. I love when you bottom out inside me and fuck me so hard I think we're gonna break the headboard."

I grabbed her hair in my fist. "You're such a naughty girl. That was dangerous. We're not doing that again."

She pouted. "But didn't it feel amazing? I loved every second of it. How you took me rough and hard, like you wanted to break me."

"Of course it felt awesome. But my love, we don't need an oops like Nolan and Avery."

"I told you, I'm on the pill. It's fine."

I yanked her hair back again. "Not again, you hear me?"

"Yes..." she whispered, but it ended in a moan. I didn't know what had gotten into her tonight, but she was all horned up, and I intended to take advantage of that.

I flipped her onto her back. "Spread 'em," I ordered.

"What are you going to do to me?" she asked, but did as I ordered, like the good girl I wanted her to be. She knew when I wanted the brat and when I needed obedience.

I grinned at her as I reached into the bedside table drawer for the wrist and ankle restraints. "You know, naughty girl. Gotta teach you a lesson."

"What lesson?"

"That you don't rile me up when I'm working, or else I get to ride this pussy rough and hard."

"So, do I get a spanking, then?" she asked gleefully.

I bound her wrists above her head first, then went to the foot of the bed and bound her ankles. "Nope, I get to watch you squirm and beg for it again."

She could only whimper in response.

I bent down so my lips were on her ear. "Now be a good girl and obey."

She nodded. "Yes, sir."

A wolfish grin spread across my face. Tonight was going to be fun.

CHAPTER FIFTEEN

LILA

"*D*ad, please pick one!" I exclaimed as I stood before him at the kitchen island with the three logo designs printed out.

I'd been home for two and a half weeks, and my dad was still hesitant to let me help him make decisions. Felix gave us these designs last week, and he had asked me what was going on. Not having the logo done meant Declan couldn't finish the website redesign. Which meant Felix couldn't design a new menu or the sign above the door.

Dad pinned me with an annoyed look from over his cup of coffee. "Honey, let me have my coffee first."

"No, make a decision!"

He glared at me. "Why are you still here?"

"I told you!" I exclaimed. "The bar's important to me. I want to help you and Mom make it successful again. We can finish the website and menu redesign if you pick a design."

He sighed. "I like the harp."

"He's worried about the name change," Mom said, coming into the kitchen to refill her cup of coffee.

"Okay," I said and nodded, understanding his concerns. "I get that. The PR firm I hired recommended doing a Grand Re-Opening. We switch everything over and do a big event to announce it."

"When?" Dad asked.

"They recommended it right away," I said.

Dad sipped his coffee as he thought about it. "You don't agree."

I tapped my fingers against the counter as I thought. "I was talking to Gemma, and maybe we should wait until Old Man Sullivan comes out."

Dad chuckled. "I love that beer name!"

Mom smiled as she stood beside me and looked at the logos again. "It's the harp, hon. It's the best one."

"I think we switch everything over now, and when the beer's done, we'll do a big release in conjunction with the brewery. It helps both our businesses."

Dad pinned me with a suspicious look. "Honey, I love that you came here to help, but you're not going to stick around waiting for that. You have to go home and get a new job, right?"

I took a sip of my coffee, hoping he wouldn't badger me about this again. Dad kept asking how long I planned to stick around, whereas Mom kept sending me links to houses for sale and apartments to rent in Drakesville.

"Maybe she wants to stay, hon," Mom said with a twinkle in her eye.

She had been mentioning that a lot lately. It didn't help that I was spending so much time with Declan, and she was getting ideas that we were back together. Although, the idea of going back hadn't been appealing to me. My focus was on getting the bar back on its feet and nothing else. I hadn't given any thought to what I wanted to do past that.

"Lila?" my dad asked.

"I'm not sure. I don't have a job right now, so I'm focused on helping you."

I wasn't going to tell him I wasn't sure I wanted to be a lawyer anymore. Or that I was seriously considering buying the bar. I had a lot of capital. I hadn't been investing my money other than purchasing my big house out West. Buying the family bar and making sure it was running smoothly was the perfect solution. But I wasn't sure my dad would go for it. The stubborn Irish man was too proud.

Mom squeezed my arm. "We love that you came home to help us, but you have your own career to worry about."

I waved her away. "Mom, I worked eighty hours a week with nothing to show for it and a fiancé who cheated on me. I'd rather be here."

Dad frowned. "Okay, but take the day off. We appreciate you picking up the slack, but that's not your job."

"Fine," I muttered and walked into the kitchen to finish my coffee. Dad went to get a shower, but Mom slid into the seat across from me at the table.

I ignored her while I drank my coffee and typed out an email to Felix.

Hey,

FINALLY have an answer! We're going with number two, and keep the text as is. We're going to do the name change, so we'll want the new logo on the new menu design. Love it so much, Fe. Thanks so much. Send me the invoice for the rest of the work, and I'll pay it right away.

-L

I shot off a text to Declan.

ME: *Felix will send you the hi-res of the logo soonish I hope.*

DECLAN: *What did we land on?*

ME: *Harp and the name change.*

DECLAN: *Perfect. Want to have lunch with me today?*

ME: *Sure, I'll see you later.*

"How long do you think you'll be here?" Mom asked.

I shrugged. "Maybe through Halloween, so another couple of weeks."

Mom smiled. "You love Halloween!"

"The kids asked if I'd take them trick or treating, and Gemma's putting together a big Halloween Party at the brewery."

I was excited about the party at the brewery. Despite Declan calling her such a PITA, Gemma and I had become fast friends since I'd been here. He said she was annoying, but I thought he loved her like a little sister. She could be quite excitable, but that was her charm.

"Hmm," was all Mom said as she sipped her coffee.

"What?"

That was some passive-aggressive Irish Mom crap if I ever heard it.

"Do you want to go back?" she asked.

"Well...I have a house, so I kinda have to," I said unconvincingly.

In the heart of my heart, deep down, if I was being one hundred percent honest with myself, I knew going home would be painful. It would be like ripping my heart from my chest when I left. I wasn't sure I could handle it again.

Mom peered at me over her coffee cup with a waiting glance. It was that 'mom look' when she wanted me to spit out what was on my mind. I knew that look, and I wasn't going to participate.

"Lila..." she said in a warning tone.

"What?"

"Have you even applied to any new jobs?"

I shook my head. "No."

"Why not? Honey, you can't live on your savings."

Well, I probably could, but my mortgage on the house in Palo Alto was astronomical, so I'd need to downsize. I had a lot of experience under my belt, so I knew I could land at another firm quickly. But I wasn't sure I wanted to be a lawyer anymore.

"Lila, do you not want to be a lawyer anymore?" Mom asked.

I looked up at her in shock. How she knew what I was thinking was beyond me.

"I don't know..."

"Well, what *do* you want to do?"

"I want to buy the bar," I admitted.

Mom looked stunned at my confession. She sat back in her chair and stared at me for a couple of seconds. It looked like she was taking a little time to process it.

"What would that mean?" she asked.

I shrugged. "I'm not sure, but I want the bar to stay in the family. I have the capital to do it."

"Would you move back?"

I could buy the bar and let my parents or Brian continue to manage it as they saw fit. I could go back to California and find a new job and move on with my life. But when I thought about doing that, I wasn't sure that was what I wanted. When I first came to town, that was definitely the idea. Now, I wasn't so sure.

"Not sure. What do you think about that?"

Mom took a sip of her coffee as she thought about it. "You're gonna need to convince your father. But...if that's what you want to do with your money, I'm okay with that."

"I need to think about it," I admitted.

She nodded, but the conversation abruptly stopped when my dad came back into the kitchen dressed for work at the bar. He and my mom left to open the bar while I looked at my finances.

The truth was, I felt more fulfilled by waiting tables the past couple of weeks than being in the courtroom. Or drafting up cease and desist letters. Or countersuits. I had a lot of things to think about, none of which I was ready to deal with. There was one reason I was thinking about a career change. I just wasn't sure it was a good idea to uproot my life for a man.

CHAPTER SIXTEEN

DECLAN

"What do you think?" I asked Lila as she stared at my computer screen in shock.

"You did all of this?" she asked.

I nodded. "Yeah, it's what you wanted, right?"

My web design skills had significantly improved since high school when I made that website for her parents' bar. This redesign had been tough, but it looked so much better. I had worked my ass off getting this done for her. Felix pushed all his projects to the side to finalize the logo and work on the wooden sign at my request.

Maybe I should have stalled him and asked him to tell her it would take a while. Since she told Felix they wanted the harp design, I felt her pulling away. She said she was going to stay through Halloween, but that was fast approaching.

"What do you think?" I repeated my question, shaking my morose thoughts away.

She closed the lid of my laptop, and when she looked up at me, she had a big smile on her face. "I love it!"

"Really?"

Her brow furrowed. "Did you think I wouldn't?"

I rubbed the back of my neck. "I wanted you to like it. How are things going at the bar?"

"Good! We have a full staff now, so I don't have to pick up shifts, but I've been trying to get my dad to take some time off so I can help with the other stuff."

Hmm, if she was leaving, that didn't make sense. That sounded like she was in it for the long haul. A part of me wanted to ask her to stay for good. I still loved Lila with every fiber of my being, but it was unfair of me to ask her to uproot her life and move back to our tiny town.

"What's that?" she asked as she saw the sign on my kitchen table wrapped in tissue paper.

"The sign."

Her eyes went wide. "Felix finished the sign, already? I told him he could take his time!"

"I wanted to show your dad tonight."

She put her hands to her chest and looked up at me with so much love and adoration. "Aw, Dec, are you nervous about dinner with my parents tonight?"

"I feel like I'm sixteen again. I want your dad to like the website and what Felix did with the sign."

She got up from her seat and wrapped her arms around my neck. She gave me a quick kiss. "It's just my dad, plus he loves you."

I wasn't sure about that. I thought he felt sorry for me after his daughter left me broken-hearted. I didn't know what he thought of me now, especially since she barely left my bed this past week. Not that I minded. I loved having her here. I had to get my fill of her before she was gone.

She cupped my face. "He'll love it. Now let's go before my sister asks if we're done fucking."

I slid my hands down her tight body and grabbed her luscious ass in my hands. "We could do that..."

She slapped my hands away. "Later, baby. Let's go!"

I grabbed my computer and the wooden sign, and we walked out of my apartment. It was a crisp fall evening, a rare one where I actually was home for a normal dinner time. When Lila said her parents wanted to invite me for dinner, I couldn't say no.

I slid my hand in hers, and we walked the block to her childhood home. When she opened the door, the smell of a good home-cooked meal wafted toward us. Lila's mom was an excellent cook; it had been a long time since I'd been in this house for one of her meals. I spent a lot of time here as a kid after my parents died. The Sullivans had been great to me, especially when my brother worked nights at their bar trying to keep food on the table for us.

"Auntie Lila! Uncle Declan!" Cora squealed excitedly when she saw us. She immediately ran over to Lila.

"Sweetie," Kelsey said as she walked into the front room to greet us. "We talked about this. Declan isn't your uncle."

"Not yet," muttered Brian from behind her.

Lila fixed him with a glare, and I pretended I hadn't heard that. It wouldn't have been the first time someone in Lila's family asked if we were back together. Cora kept asking us when we were going to give her a cousin.

"Lemme go find your dad," I said to Lila.

She nodded, preoccupied with listening intently to her niece's story. I found Sean Sullivan in the living room watching the Bulldogs game.

"Declan, come sit!" he called to me.

I sat on the couch next to him and set the wooden sign

next to me while I opened my laptop. "I showed Lila first, but I wanted to get your blessing since you're the owner."

"Ah, she's the moneybags," he joked and took a swig of his beer. A sense of pride coursed through me that he was drinking one of my brewery's beers.

I opened the demo site where I had built out the website design. I pointed to my screen. "Okay, I updated the new logo everywhere and added the new photos. I wanted it to be a clean design, so it looks new and exciting for your customers."

He shrugged. "Looks good to me."

"You sure?"

He nodded. "If Lila's good with it, I'm good with it. Between you and me, I think she's vying for my job."

I closed my laptop and put it on the coffee table. Brian walked into the living room with two beers and handed one to me. I couldn't ask Sean what he meant about Lila and his job because Brian eyed the sign next to me and asked, "What's that?"

"Oh!" I exclaimed. "Felix did the woodwork and painting for the logo."

"Let's see it," Sean said.

I set down my beer and unwrapped the sign from the tissue paper. I had been impressed that Felix turned around the work so quickly, but I had asked him to make it a priority. Gemma probably said something too.

I held it up in front of me and showed Sean, then Brian. They both nodded their approval.

"It looks great!" Sean said.

I nodded. "Good. I know Lila had to sell you on the logo, but I think it's really good, and it'll help with the rebrand."

"Pops, Lila's gonna take your job, huh?" Brian joked.

I frowned. What were they talking about?

I grabbed my beer and took a swig.

"Maybe," Sean said. He gave me a quizzical look. "If she stays."

"What do you mean?" I asked.

Brian raised an eyebrow at me. "Maybe you can convince her to stay this time, bud."

I shook my head. No. I wasn't doing that. Lila had a life in California, a life she built up after going across the country to an amazing college. I wasn't letting her sacrifice her career to come back to this town. To what, be a waitress?

Brian rolled his eyes. "Pops, he doesn't know."

"Know what?" I asked and eyed both of them suspiciously.

"I still want to sell," Sean admitted.

My face fell. After all the work Lila had done for her family's bar, her dad still wanted to sell it off?

"To my daughter, dummy," he said.

I opened my mouth in surprise. "Oh."

I wanted to ask what that meant, but then Kelly called us in for dinner.

Before we went in, Sean put a hand on my arm. "Declan, maybe you could get her to stay this time. She had a good reason to go before, and you're a good man for letting her chase her dreams, but maybe it's time for her to come home."

"I..." I wasn't sure what he was trying to say to me.

He squeezed my arm. "I know you and my daughter still love each other. It would be a shame to let her slip through your fingers again."

I stood there with my mouth flopping open like a fish, unsure what all that meant. I didn't want her to leave. Of course I didn't, but I didn't think there was ever a possibility that she would stay. Why was her family pushing? Did they know something I didn't?

I brushed it off when Lila came into the living room. She put her hands on her hips and gave me an exasperated look. "Did you get lost? Come get dinner with the rest of us."

I grabbed my beer. "I'm coming."

"Maybe later." She winked at me and spun on her heel into the other room.

I shook my head at her and hoped she was right.

I walked into the kitchen and took my seat next to Lila at the table. Her parents sat at each end, with Brian and Kelsey across from us. Callie was in her high chair while Cora was sitting on her mom's lap.

"Declan, I'm so glad you made it," her mom said.

"Thanks for having me," I told her.

"You're always welcome," she told me. "Eat everyone!"

We all started piling up our plates with vegetables, mashed potatoes, and slices of the roast Kelly had made. I slid my hand on Lila's thigh underneath the table while I ate with my other hand. She smiled, hiding it behind her beer bottle.

I listened to Brian and Sean argue about the Bulldogs; it was like being at my brother's house. Nolan and I had similar arguments over the sport we loved. Lila shook her head at their antics, but she looked right at home at her parents' house with me beside her.

"Oh, did we decide on doing a grand re-opening?" Brian asked Lila.

Lila shrugged. "I don't know."

"Do it next weekend! We could have a big party," Kelsey said.

Lila pushed her peas around on her plate. "We should probably do it with the beer release."

"But you'll be back in California by then, right?" Kelsey asked.

Lila shrugged and put her fork in her mouth so she didn't have to answer.

"I think we should do it now," Brian agreed. "I could get Finn to see if his band can play."

"You don't have to wait for the beer to be done," I suggested. "You could do the big grand re-opening to let people know about the name change, and then we'll do a joint beer release party. I'll talk to Gemma."

Lila's eyes lit up when she looked up at me. "You will?"

I nodded. "Don't worry, it'll be great."

"Do it before you go home," Sean chimed in.

Lila nodded. "Okay..."

"You're gonna stay through Halloween, right?" Kelsey asked.

"Auntie Lila said she'd take me trick or treating!" Cora chimed in.

"She did?" Brian asked his daughter.

Lila smiled back at her niece. "I promised, and I don't go back on my word."

"Then next week, because the following week's the Halloween party at the brewery," Kelsey said.

"Why? Are you worried about competing?" Lila asked.

"Sorta," Brian said. "Bar's still busy the weekend before Halloween, especially since it's on a Monday this year, but I'd prefer to do something unrelated to the holiday."

"Does that give us enough time to plan?" Kelly asked nervously.

"We got the sign made, the new menus printed, and if we get entertainment, that should be good," Lila said firmly.

"I'll start figuring out how to advertise it, and then we set a time."

Sean grinned at his daughter. "Sounds like you got it all figured out."

"You got the sign made?" Kelly asked.

Lila turned to me. "Go get it and show my mom."

I pushed my chair out from the table and retrieved it from the living room. When I walked back into the kitchen, I held up the sign so they all could see.

Kelly had a grin from ear to ear. "I love it!"

"It's good work," Sean agreed.

"Love it," Kelsey chimed in, while Brian nodded in agreement.

I handed it to Lila. "Well, I think you can have this now, so you can hang it up above the door."

She gave me a bright smile and squeezed my hand.

We were about to finish dinner, so I cleared my and Lila's plates and started helping clean up.

"You're a guest!" Kelly insisted as she walked into the kitchen. "You don't have to do that. God knows my children didn't lift a finger to help."

I noticed Lila and her sister had disappeared, as did Brian and Sean. That was fine. I didn't mind helping clean up. It was nice that the Sullivans invited me. But I had to admit, dinner felt like a weird blast from the past.

"The sign looks good," Kelly said to me while she wiped down the counter and I put the dishes away.

"Felix is an amazing artist. He does all of our artwork. I had to push him to pursue it on the side."

She gave me a curious look. "You're good at pushing people into what they should do, huh?"

I shrugged. I guessed that was true. I saw potential with

both Felix and Gemma for different reasons, and pushed them to pursue it.

"Well, maybe you can push my daughter to move home."

"I don't know..."

"Declan, if she has a reason to stay, she will. Be her reason."

I didn't know what I was supposed to say to that, but it was interesting that both of Lila's parents were pushing me to get their daughter to move back. I understood why Lila left. I left for college too, but I came back. Drakesville was my home, but it wasn't hers. Not anymore.

Kelly took two pies out of the fridge. "I know you love apple, so I got you some of that."

"Mrs. Sullivan, you didn't have to do that."

"Declan! You're a grown man. Please call me Kelly," she said with a laugh.

I laughed too. Some habits were hard to break.

"Or maybe one day you can call me Mom."

I rubbed the back of my neck. "Umm..."

"What? My daughter has been sleeping at your place since practically the first night she got here."

I felt my face get hot with embarrassment. Okay, true, but I didn't want her parents to think about all the sex we were having.

She laughed in my face. "Oh, honey, I don't care about that. You two are adults, but maybe..."

"Maybe, what?"

"Maybe you finally found your way back to each other."

"I wish that was the case, but she's got a life to go back to."

Kelly pursed her lips and put the pies on the dining room table. I went to get the plates and brought them over to the table. Kelly walked into the living room, and I heard her yelling at everyone else for dessert.

When she came back in, she gave my arm a little squeeze. "Think about it, honey. You're meant for each other. I know it."

I thought about it all throughout dessert. While I was the lone one who ate apple pie and the rest of the family was content with classic pumpkin. Lila's mom didn't have to do that for me, but it was nice she had been so kind.

I thought about what she said when I kissed Lila on the doorstep, like I used to when we were teenagers.

"You okay?" Lila asked.

I nodded.

"Sorry, I'd come with you, but Cora wants to do a sleepover with Auntie Lila," she said with a roll of her eyes, but secretly she loved being the fun aunt.

I brushed her hair behind her ear. "S'okay, love. I've held you hostage enough. Spend time with your family."

"You're so good to me. I'll see you later. This week will be busy with planning the party," Lila said.

"I know. I'm here if you need me."

"You're the best, Dec. Goodnight."

I gave her one last lingering kiss, and then I walked home.

I thought about stopping at my brother's to talk to him, but he would have said I told you so. I was deeply in love with Lila Sullivan, and I knew she was going to break my heart again. Even if she bought her parents' bar, I didn't think she would stay. I hadn't been enough for her back then and wouldn't be enough now. No matter what her parents thought. What Lila and I had was only for this moment, and when she finally left, it would be over again. I just hoped my heart could handle it this time.

CHAPTER SEVENTEEN

LILA

*P*lanning a last-minute Grand Re-Opening was a lot of work. I felt like I only got to sneak in a couple of hours of time with Declan this week as we rushed around to get everything ready for the event.

Brian's brother Finn played fiddle in a Celtic band, so they would be our live entertainment. Finn and Killian were like night and day, and they hated each other, so that was interesting to deal with. I was glad I only had one sister. If there were three other Kelseys, we might have tried to kill each other. Brian joked that was why they had a reputation for being the 'Fighting Murphys.'

I felt bad I barely got to see Declan this week since I was organizing the event and helping pick up the slack. I'd make it up to him next week, especially since next weekend was Halloween. I had to come up with a sexy costume for the party at the brewery and make sure he knew how much I appreciated him. I wondered why that even mattered. We were just fucking. He wasn't my boyfriend.

Brian rushed into the back office, where I was counting the drawer and making sure we weren't under. He looked like he had been pulling out his hair. The dinner rush was about to start, and I had been at the bar all day picking up the slack while Brian was dealing with deliveries.

"What's wrong?" I asked.

His jaw ticked in annoyance. "Fucking Killian called out."

Shit. I wasn't much of a bartender. I could handle getting someone a beer, but mixed drinks, not so much. You would be surprised how many people came to an Irish bar and ordered a Manhattan.

"I pulled Sarah to the bar since she's bartended before, but can you take some tables?"

"Let me finish counting this," I said.

"So...you sure you want to buy this place?" he asked.

"I want the bar to stay in the family."

He nodded in agreement. "I can't afford to buy it."

"I know, but if I do, I still want you to manage it. I'd just be the owner."

He crossed his arms as he studied me. "So what? You'll help us get up to speed, buy the bar, and then leave again?"

I shrugged and finished counting the money and put it into the safe. "Not sure yet, but whatever my ownership status will be, I'll draw up a contract, so we have everything in writing."

"Seriously?"

"Yes, seriously!" I exclaimed and looked at him like he had two heads.

Then I remembered that was a lawyer thing to say. I had been working as a lawyer for so long that I forgot places like this weren't so insistent on getting everything on paper. But I knew how things backfired when not having stuff in writing. I'd draw up a contract no matter what.

"Such a lawyer," Brian joked.

"Shut it!"

He grinned.

I grabbed my pad of paper and pen and walked out onto the floor. Sarah, my dad, and my mom were all behind the bar. It was the middle of happy hour, and the dinner rush was swarming in, so the bar was packed. I felt like it hadn't been this packed in a while.

I watched a couple of the other servers weave in and out of the floor as they got drinks and food delivered to their tables. I checked the host stand for Sarah's section, then went over to get table twelve their dinner order. Brian must have sat them and got their drinks already.

"Hi, I'm Lila. I'll be serving you tonight. What can I get you?" I asked as soon as I got there.

Mr. Davies and his wife were sitting at the table, and they gave me a big smile. "Lila, what are you doing waiting tables again?"

"Just helping out. We had someone call out sick. What can I get you?"

"Tell us about the grand re-opening tomorrow," Mrs. Davies said.

"Oh!" I exclaimed. "We're changing up the menu, and we're renaming the bar, so we wanted to do a big celebration. We'll have some great specials and a Celtic band in the evening playing music."

"Oh, that sounds like fun!" she said. "We should come back."

"You should!" I said with a smile.

Maybe if enough people asked, and I was enthusiastic enough, they'd come out tomorrow. I was banking on it to help us pull ourselves up by our bootstraps. I didn't want to go home with the bar still in dire straits.

"What are you changing on the menu?" Mr. Davies asked.

"You'll have to come tomorrow and find out," I said cheekily.

They both laughed.

"Tell us, dear," Mrs. Davies began. "How's the Irish beef stew?"

"Amazing! It's made with Guinness, so it has a rich flavor to it. We also have a potato or beef pasty with a side salad if you want comfort food. I love that," I explained.

"Oh, I think I want to do the stew," she said. "It's something different."

I took her menu away. "What about you, Mr. Davies?"

He pored over the menu for a second. "Ah, give me the Drakesville Burger. I'm a simple man."

"You got it!"

I took his menu away and rushed to put their order in. It was picking up, and the rest of the night was a frenzy as I hopped from table to table, taking care of our customers. Many had questions about tomorrow's event, but they seemed interested. Waiting tables could be a thankless job, but tonight I was thriving. Everyone in town kept asking me how I was doing, making me miss living in a small town like this. Sure, people were nosy, but maybe I had been wrong to stay away for so long.

There was a bit of a lull after the dinner rush, but after ten, it picked up again as people came out for drinks. Or they were bar hopping. There was a bar on the other side of town. It was kind of divey, but sometimes you'd find college kids doing a bar crawl. They'd go to Drakesville Tavern,

The MacGregor Brothers Brewing Company, and then to us.

Working my tail off at the bar made me remember how much I loved this job as a teenager. I don't think that was strictly legal, but no one in town cared since my dad owned the place. I should have wanted to go back to my life as a big-time lawyer for a fortune five hundred company, but I didn't want to do any of that. That should scare me, but it didn't.

"Hey, stranger," a familiar deep voice said as they parked themselves on one of the barstools.

I turned and gave Declan a big smile, which slid right off my face when I realized what time it was. I put my hands in my hair in frustration. Unlike the brewery, we were open until two a.m., so Declan had already closed the brewery for the night since it was a little past midnight.

"Oh my god, I'm so sorry!" I told him.

He smiled but held up his hand when my dad offered him a beer. "I'm good, thanks, though."

Dad tilted his head towards the door. "Go on, you've done enough for today."

"I need to cash out."

Dad nodded. "Excuse us, Declan."

Dad and I went into the back office, where I cashed out for the night.

"I think tomorrow's gonna go well," I told him. "Lots of people asked me about it."

He nodded. "I hope so."

"Dad, I want the bar to stay in the family. All my recommendations have been to do that."

"I know, honey. I love that you wanted to help out. You've helped us more than you know, but it wasn't just the finances that made me want to sell."

"No?" I asked. That was all my mom had said, that the bottom line was suffering, and they needed to sell the building.

"I want to retire. I want to spend time with my grandkids, and I couldn't leave Brian in charge with the finances being such a mess."

I nodded. "We'll figure it out so you can retire."

I wasn't ready to ask him if he'd sell me the bar. I needed to take baby steps. Talking to my mom and my sister had been those first steps, but I didn't have the courage to tell my dad I wanted to be the silent partner. That I had the capital to get the bar back on its feet for good. He had gotten mad when I paid for the marketing consultants and Declan and Felix for their services.

He cashed me out, and I clocked out. I didn't want to clock in, but Dad had been strict on making sure he knew I was on the books. "Go on, get out of here," he said.

"Thanks. I didn't realize how late it was."

"You're working really hard. You don't need to do that."

"I want to. Bye, Dad, I'll see you tomorrow."

I walked back onto the floor and saw Declan and Brian chatting. I sidled up to Declan, and he smiled when he saw me approach. "Ready?" he asked.

I nodded. "Yeah, I really need a shower. I smell like Guinness."

He raised an eyebrow.

"Someone spilled their beer on me earlier. Let's go. Bye Bri, I'll see you tomorrow."

🍁

"Oh my god, that feels amazing," I moaned as Declan sat behind me and rubbed my bare shoulders.

We were cuddling in his bed after we had showered and had sex. After he undid the restraints, I complained about my aching body, and he immediately offered to give me a massage. This man, I swear.

He kissed my shoulder. "You're working so hard. Tell me what you need."

I pulled his arms around my waist and leaned back against him. "This is perfect, thanks."

He leaned back against the headboard of his bed, and we settled into each other. "Are you ready for tomorrow?"

I nodded. "I think so. I roped all of Brian's brothers into helping us. I'm pretty pissed Killian called out today, so he better show up."

He kissed the side of my neck. "You better crack the whip."

I laughed. "Brian keeps calling me the boss, but I don't know."

"What don't you know?"

I sighed and moved away from him, sitting next to him with my back against the headboard. "I want to buy the bar."

"Okay," he said without a hint of emotion. Like he already knew.

"I want it to stay in the family, but tonight my dad said something about wanting to retire. I feel like that's a sign I should do it."

"What would that mean?"

I shrugged.

I wanted to save the bar. That was why I had been here for the past several weeks getting the website redesigned, the logo redone, and hiring a marketing person to help me figure out social media. When I first came back to Drakesville, I thought I wanted to buy the bar and be the silent partner. That I'd make sure our finances were in good shape, and then I'd go home, but now I wasn't so sure. Part of the reason was sitting beside me.

"If you bought the bar, would you stay?" he asked.

I wanted so badly for him to beg me to stay. To tell me to change my whole career path and stay with him forever. But he wasn't doing that. If I stayed, I wasn't sure where that left us. I heard some whispers about Declan lately. Maybe he just wanted a temporary fling. If I moved back and he didn't want a relationship, that would have been embarrassing.

"I'm not sure, but I have to ask my dad if he'll let me first."

"Okay, let's not make any big decisions tonight. You have a long day tomorrow, so let's get some sleep."

I got out of bed and slipped on one of his t-shirts. I was tall, but Declan was taller and lankier. His shirts slid down my body like a dress. He got up and put on a clean pair of boxers and then glared at me when my clothes were still left on the floor. He could be so anal about things needing to be tidy.

"It wouldn't kill you to have my jeans on the floor!" I said with a laugh.

He passive-aggressively threw my dirty clothes in his hamper. I was still laughing when I slipped down under the comforter.

He turned off the lights and slid in behind me. "You're doing amazing with the bar. Tomorrow's gonna be great."

I hadn't told him how nervous I was about tomorrow. I wanted everything to succeed. "You're coming, right?"

He cupped my face. "Love, I told you I would. I wouldn't miss it for the world. And then after that's done, the following weekend, we have the Halloween party, so you can relax."

"Oh, I need to get a costume."

He grinned. "Something really sexy."

I laughed. "Of course! You better wear one too. You can't be boring!"

He silenced me with a goodnight kiss. "We'll figure it out."

I noticed he didn't ask me again when I was leaving. I hadn't booked a return flight home yet, but 'After Halloween' wasn't a real timeframe. We had been avoiding talking about it because that meant our time was running out. I didn't want to think about a life where I wasn't sleeping beside the man I loved.

That's how I knew I was in trouble with Declan MacGregor. He was the only man I had ever loved, and I was contemplating moving back to Drakesville. But that was completely ridiculous. Wasn't it?

CHAPTER EIGHTEEN

DECLAN

Saturdays were always a busy day at the brewery. For one, it was the weekend, and two, Nolan and I usually put in a lot of hours on the weekend. Before he married Avery, it was common for us to both work from open to close. Since Lila blew back into my life, I hadn't been doing that anymore, which wasn't a bad thing.

One of the most important things we did on Saturdays was to look at the numbers and make sure we were on track. Nolan wasn't big on numbers. He left the business side of the brewery up to me. Which worked because I didn't know shit about brewing beer.

"I'm only going to work a half day," I said to him afterward.

Nolan leaned back in his chair and stroked his beard as he studied me. "That's not like you."

"I want to go over and help Lila set up for the grand re-opening party."

Nolan nodded. "Ah. That makes sense."

We stared at each other for a couple of seconds, both challenging each other to say what was really on our minds. My brother could be a grump, but since he got married, he had been pushing me to take time off. Now he seemed like he had a problem with it.

"We should close the brewery early," he said.

I raised my eyebrows at his suggestion. Nolan didn't make it a secret that he didn't like that Lila and I were doing whatever we were doing, so that surprised me.

"Why?"

"To support the Sullivans," he said. "Dec, Kelly and Sean helped us so much after Mom and Dad died."

I nodded. While Nolan was busy working and trying to make things work with his then-wife Kath, I spent a lot of time at Lila's house. We had been best friends, but all that time I spent with her over the years while my brother struggled to raise me had cemented our connection. That's why I was completely gutted when she walked out of my life.

"Can we do that?" I asked. "Close the brewery early?"

Nolan looked at me like I was the dumbest person on the planet. "Bro, we're the owners. We can do what we want."

"I don't want to cut our staff's wages," I explained.

One thing I tried so hard to do was make sure everyone was paid fairly here and with respect. Closing the brewery without alerting our staff was a dick move.

Nolan seemed to take in my argument. "Okay, fair. But I'm already planning to go over with Avery."

"With the baby?"

"Hell no!" he exclaimed, and then he looked guilty. He rubbed a big hand down his beard. "That makes me sound like an ass. I love my daughter, she and Avery are the best things that ever happened to me, but we need a break. Avery's dad is taking her for the night."

"How's Avery taking that?" I asked. Avery had a hard time when she went back to school this fall after being on maternity leave all summer.

"I told her we're gonna get drunk and bang all night," he said with a grin. "But honestly, we'll probably have one beer and go home to sleep in peace."

I laughed. "Should have thought of that before you knocked her up."

That got me the middle-finger salute.

I went back to my computer, but I noticed Nolan hadn't left to check on the hops yet. "What?" I asked.

"Lila's stuck around for a while, huh?"

"She's still going back."

"When, though?"

I shrugged. "Sometime after Halloween, but..."

"What?"

"She said something last night about wanting to buy the bar from her dad and how he wants to retire."

Nolan stroked his beard. "You think that would make her stay?"

"I don't know."

Nolan sighed. "Fuck."

"What?"

"You love her."

"Yeah?"

That wasn't a secret. Nolan bugged me constantly about being so hung up on her. He knew I still loved Lila, and I knew that was still true after these past couple of weeks with adult Lila. She owned me, body and soul, and no one would ever compare to her.

"Bro, she's going to break your heart again."

I waved him off. "Stay out of it. I'm not a little kid anymore who you can tell what to do. I'm a grown-ass adult who can make his own decisions."

Nolan held up his hands to me in surrender. "Okay, okay. I want you to have what Avery and I have."

I nodded.

I wanted that too. Pretty sure who I wanted that with, but Lila and I were two ships passing in the night. It was fun for now, but we'd never be on the same page. Or rather, the same town. Or even state. My life was here. Nolan and I built our brewery from the ground up, and I was never leaving Pennsylvania. Lila was only staying long enough to make sure Sean didn't sell the family bar. It would never work out.

"Can you go away now?" I asked, fixing my brother with a glare. "I have shit I need to do, and you're hovering."

He stomped off in typical Nolan grumpiness, and I went back to finishing up the day's work.

Before I left, I talked with Wyatt to make sure he had everything he needed, but he was fine closing without me. Asher was behind the bar with him to close because Felix asked to switch since he and Gemma were going over to Sullivan's too.

I walked over to the bar and found Lila ordering people around. She looked so in a zone, like she belonged there telling everyone what to do. Like she was already the owner. Her eyes lit up when she saw me.

"Hey, what are you doing here?" she asked after she gave me a quick kiss.

"I'm here to help. Where do you want me?"

"Probably naked in her bed," Kelsey muttered as she walked by me.

Lila glared in her sister's direction. "She's been crabby

all day. Ignore her."

"Not wrong, though, right?" I teased.

She beamed at me. "Nope, but not right now. So much to do."

"Put me to work!"

She jumped into my arms, and I made an 'oof' sound as I caught her. She wrapped her arms around my neck and kissed me. I slid my hands around her waist and gripped her hips as we deepened the kiss.

I pulled away before she could deepen it further. "What was that for?"

"I missed you, and I love that you're willing to help."

I twirled a dark strand of her hair in between my fingers. "Of course, love. Tell me what to do."

Sullivan's bar...ahem, now Sullivan's Irish Pub was packed way more than I had ever seen in my entire life. And that was saying something because I spent a lot of time here growing up.

It was loud in here, with people drunkenly chatting and the loud sounds of the fiddle and singing coming from the front of the room. I didn't know the name of Finn Murphy's band, but they were pretty good. Think of any stereotypical traditional Celtic band, and that was exactly their vibe. With his bright shock of red hair and green kilt, he looked like a freaking stereotype. Finn played the fiddle with gusto while a tiny redheaded woman sang her lungs out in front of him.

"I thought kilts were a Scottish thing," Gemma said as she stared at Finn from her seat next to me at the bar.

Felix shrugged. "I don't know. Ask the Scottish-American next to you."

I shrugged. "It's all Celtic. So who cares?"

Gemma nodded in approval as she looked around the pub. "No, I get it, it's a gimmick, and it definitely works. It matches the vibe here. Lila did a great job putting this together so fast. I'm impressed."

I nodded and sipped my beer. Killian and Brian were behind the bar, slinging back beers and looking stressed, but in a good way. In a way, that told me the place hadn't been this packed in a really long time.

Lila had been taking tables since it was so busy that I saw spare glimpses of her every once in a while, but I let her do her thing. She seemed to thrive on being at the pub, and a part of me wondered if I could convince her to stay. If not for me, but for her family's business. After all the work she put into the place, was she really going to up and leave?

"When does Lila go back to California?" Felix asked.

I shrugged. "She keeps saying vaguely after Halloween."

Gemma put her hand on her chin. "Okay. That means I need to make sure the Halloween party's the best damn one we've ever thrown."

I waved her off. "It'll be great. You already did so much planning."

Gemma pulled out her phone and started tapping away at something. Felix gave her an annoyed look, but she ignored him as she focused on her phone.

Felix told me when they had been in the Poconos together before Gemma accepted the marketing director job, she had thought of marketing stuff for the brewery the whole time. She took photos for the social channels and even took him on some brewery tours, where she compared our beers. She never stopped thinking about what to do to help the brewery. That had been exactly why I wanted her for the job in the first place.

"Sweet thing," Felix said in a warning tone. "We agreed not to do work stuff tonight. It's our night out."

She held up a finger to him. "One second."

He bent down towards her ear and whispered something that made a blush blossom across Gemma's face. I didn't want to know, but I had a feeling it was super dirty.

I looked around to see if Avery and Nolan were still around, but they were nowhere in sight.

Gemma slid her phone back into her pocket. "Oh, those two bounced like an hour ago. You were too busy drooling over your girl."

"Shut it!" I said and nudged her arm.

"Truth, though," she teased.

Felix hid his smile behind his beer glass.

Traitor.

Speaking of the devil, Lila came up behind the bar and punched something into the register. She gave me a tight smile. "One more table, and then we can go."

"You do what you need to do," I told her. "I'll be right here waiting."

She leaned over the bar and gave me a quick kiss. She bent to my ear. "I'm going to let you fuck my face so hard later."

I nearly choked at that, and I was pretty sure Gemma and Felix heard what she said based on their snickering beside me. Lila grinned like the little brat she was and walked off.

Gemma nudged me.

"Not a word," I snapped.

She grinned. "No wonder you've been in such a good mood lately."

"Lay off him." Felix came to my rescue.

"Well, Lila certainly hasn't."

I sipped my beer and tried to ignore her. She was right, though. Since Lila swooped back into my life, I had been in a better mood. I didn't work twelve hours days at the brewery anymore. I was better at my work-life balance. When she left, that was going to change. I'd bury myself in my work again to forget the woman I loved left me again.

Gemma and Felix left shortly after, but I stayed until close with Lila waiting for her to be done. She was basically managing the place with Brian already. I couldn't imagine her buying the bar and then going back to her life in California. But wouldn't she have told me she was thinking of moving back?

"Get out of here," Brian told her as they cashed out the drawer. "Killian and I will close the pub, okay? You've done enough."

"You sure?" she asked him.

Brian nodded. "Go. Your man's been sitting here waiting for you all night."

Her grin got bigger. "I know. He's the best."

I threw down a wad of cash on the bar since I had been drinking here all night and walked out of the pub with Lila. She was practically bouncing as we walked back to my apartment, despite how late it was and how tired she probably was.

"Do you think it went well?" she asked as she took off her clothes when we got upstairs and headed for the shower.

I followed behind her and shook my head at the trail of clothes she left on my floor. I loved her, but her need to be messy drove me batty. I took off my clothes, neatly folded them, and placed them on the toilet seat.

"It was great. Now, can you take a day off?" I asked as I got into the shower with her.

She gave me a cheeky grin. "And do what?"

I cupped her face. "Let's take the day and spend it in my bed."

"Wow, you took a half day, and you want to take a full day to be with me? I'm shocked," she said as she turned on the water, reaching her hand out to test the temperature.

"You're such a brat."

"You love me!" she teased and closed her eyes to get under the shower head.

I watched the water cascading down her body as she washed her hair. This was a total sexy moment, but when I looked at Lila, I thought about how fast my heart beat when she was near. How much I wanted so badly to keep her by my side.

My big, dumb heart was in so much trouble. All because my dick couldn't help himself.

Hazel eyes popped open. "Are you gonna shower or watch me?"

I smirked at her. "I don't know. You're giving me a good show."

She playfully slapped my arm. "Ass!"

We switched positions, and I washed my hair while she scrubbed the smell of deep-fried foods and beer off herself. Despite how hard my dick was at seeing her naked body wet, we were both too tired for anything more.

We toweled off together and I passive-aggressively put her dirty clothes away in my hamper. She laughed at me while she lay naked in my bed.

I crawled into bed with her.

"I was serious about earlier. Do you think it went well?" she asked. She bit her nails as she looked up at me.

"I've never seen it that packed."

She nodded. "Me either, but...I want to make sure it will last. I want..." She trailed off and raked her hand through her hair with a sigh.

"What's wrong, love?"

"I think my dad still might sell."

I hadn't mentioned that he said he wanted to sell to her. Because that came with the stipulation of her moving back home, and I didn't want to force her hand like that.

"Did you tell him you want to buy it?"

She shook her head. "Not yet. I'm worried he won't let me."

I cupped her face. "Let's not worry about it right now. How about we get some sleep?"

Her eyes popped out of her head. "Really? You want to sleep? I thought you'd want to ravish me into the wee hours of the morning."

I turned off the light and pulled her against my chest. I brushed her hair off her shoulder and pressed a small kiss on her skin. "No. I'm taking tomorrow off. I have all day to torture you with my tongue."

She bit her lip and craned her head to look back at me. "You really took the day off? For me?"

I nodded. "I knew you'd be exhausted. Plus, I only have a little more time left with you. I want to make it count."

She turned back to face the wall, and I knew she was thinking about how time was running out for us. I didn't mean to upset her by saying that, but it was the reality. While this thing between us had been fun, I knew it wasn't forever.

"Let's make it count," she whispered.

I put my lips to her ear. "Oh, I fully intend to."

CHAPTER NINETEEN

LILA

"Is this too slutty?" I asked my sister as I slid into the slinky black dress and examined myself in the mirror.

Tonight was the Halloween party at the brewery, and I wanted my costume to be sexy for Declan. We had spent as much time as we could together over the last week, but we both knew our time was coming to an end soon. Kelsey played the sister card to get me to go shopping with her today. I had been so wrapped up in Declan I forgot about a costume, so she dragged me to the mall in Green Willow.

Drakesville had a little consignment shop, but even the Target was in a different town. That was the one downside to living in a small town like this. But everything in this area was so close together that it was never a big deal to run out a few towns over for what you needed.

Kelsey cocked her head at me. "Nah, you look hot."

I shifted the shoulders of the black dress. It wasn't a costume dress, but a dress I could wear on a date. Kelsey felt like that was way more practical than buying some costume at the Halloween store I'd never wear again. The dress was low cut and had a big slit down one leg. It was sexy as hell, and I knew Declan would love it.

"It's perfect for one of those galas you always go to," she said.

She had a good point there. *If* I decided to go back to my life as a tech lawyer.

"I'm gonna get it. But we need to stop at the Halloween store so I can get a black hat."

My sister shook her head. "Nah. We have one in the bag of Halloween costumes in the attic at Mom and Dad's."

I took off the dress and put it back on the hanger. I got dressed back in my street clothes, and we walked out of the fitting room. I paid for my dress, and we got into my sister's car to head back to my parents' house.

"Did you ask Dad if you could buy the bar yet?" she asked as she drove off.

I shook my head.

That was definitely not a subject I had broached with Dad. Since the Grand Re-opening, the Pub had been hopping. It was like word got out to everyone. Maybe that was also because I was making sure to stay on top of the social media posts. Having the new website and a bigger social presence definitely helped.

It was for that reason I was hesitant. Maybe they didn't need me to buy the bar if things were turning around, but my dad said he wanted to retire. Could he retire and let Brian take over the reins?

"Would Brian be upset if I bought it?" I asked.

Kelsey shook her head. "Absolutely not. Brian loves managing the bar, but he likes that it's not his responsibility at the end of the day. If you buy it, you'll own it and have the final say. Or you can let Bri do the day-to-day that he already does. We want you to buy it."

"Why? Because you'll bully me into letting you do what you want?"

"No!" she cried. "We know you won't cut corners because you care about that bar. Although..."

I eyed my sister as we sat at the light until we turned into our parents' driveway.

"Well, what?"

She parked her car and cut the engine. "How are you gonna do that from California?"

I groaned. "I can be a silent partner. Like you said, Brian can manage it, and I can be the capital."

Kelsey shook her head. "I don't think that's gonna work for Dad. He'll only sell if he knows the person cares about the bar."

That seemed like a load of bullshit to me, but whatever.

We got out of the car and walked into the house. Kelsey was greeted by Cora and Callie running to her and screaming, 'Mommy!' I smiled at them as she let her children talk off her ear while I walked upstairs into my old room.

I laid my dress out on the bed and searched for the right shoes to wear. I found a pair of black stilettos that would look sexy with the dress. I looked in my underwear drawer for a sexy pair, then decided to be brazen and forgo them for the night. I got dressed and did my makeup, dark and witchy, with a smoky eye, and black lipstick. I was so excited for the party even though it wasn't technically Halloween. That wasn't until Monday.

When I came downstairs, my sister handed me the witch hat. She was on the floor in the living room with the girls digging through the bags of all the old costumes from when we were little.

"Oh god!" I exclaimed. "Those probably have cobwebs. You should get rid of some of them."

Mom laughed. "Not wrong. Are you going over to the brewery now?"

I nodded. "Yup. I think I have to drag someone away from their computer."

Declan hadn't been responding to my texts all day. Gemma texted me earlier that I might need to rescue him tonight, so I had a feeling he was burying himself in his work again.

"I'm probably not going to be home," I said to my parents.

"You've barely been home since you got home," Dad teased.

I felt my face get hot. It wasn't like my parents were dumb, but talking to them about sex made me want to throw up, even though they never shamed me about it and always were open about how it was healthy.

"Bye, I'll see you later!"

"You walking?" Kelsey asked.

"Yeah? It's like a block away."

"Be careful," Mom said.

"Mom, we live in a very safe town in the suburbs. I'll be fine."

"Still be careful!" both my parents said in unison.

I waved goodbye to them as I made my way over to the brewery.

As I got closer, I saw lit-up LED jack-o'-lanterns on the ground lined up as a guide to the entrance. A vampire and a fairy were walking in front of me hand-in-hand, laughing as they opened the door to the brewery. The vampire held the door open for me, and I gave him a smile in thanks. Inside, the brewery had been transformed into a Halloween spectacular.

I didn't know how Gemma did it, but it looked amazing. 'Thriller' was blaring on the stereo, and fake cobwebs hung above the bar. I spotted Gemma behind the bar dressed like a princess in a long blonde wig, and Felix was dressed as Mario. Oh! They were Mario and Princess Peach. That was adorable.

Gemma's eyes lit up when she saw me. "Hey, there you are! You look amazing!"

I gestured to my dress nonchalantly. "This old thing? The place looks awesome."

Felix nudged her. "Told you! Now go enjoy it, and get out from behind my bar. That's not your job anymore."

Gemma gave him a big smile and a quick kiss before obeying him.

"Where's Dec?" I asked.

Gemma rolled her eyes. "Still working! Give him shit for his boring costume, will you?"

I grinned at her. "I will! I'll get him to come out to the party."

"I hope so!"

I walked down the hall to the back office and frowned when it was closed, but it was unlocked. I found Declan sitting behind his computer, glasses on and his eyes glued to whatever he was working on. I looked at his 'costume' and wanted to shake him. He was wearing a skeleton t-shirt, but otherwise, no costume at all.

When I looked at him, though, I had another idea about what I wanted to do before I dragged him out to the party.

I slammed the door shut behind me and locked it for good measure.

Declan jumped at the sound, but then his eyes got dark as they scanned across my body.

"Look at you," he purred.

I strode over to him, and he arched an eyebrow up at me when I climbed on top of him. I wrapped my hands around the back of his neck and gave him an innocent look. "What about me, huh?"

Declan took off his glasses and laid them on the desk behind me. I pressed my knees into his chair, widening my stance so my thighs were pressed against his own. His eyes got darker with his arousal as he slid his hands from the top of my breasts down to my sides. "Sexy little witch."

I grinned and adjusted the pointy hat on my head. "You like?"

"Yeah, love, you put a spell on me."

He slid a hand underneath my dress, and his eyebrow shot up when he came across my bare flesh instead of lacy panties. He pressed a thumb against my clit, and I jolted at his touch. His gaze seared across my skin as he pressed those thick fingers inside me nice and slow.

"Naughty little witch not wearing any panties," he growled and pumped his fingers in and out of me.

I rocked against his hand, trying to match the friction of his touch. "Mmm. Right there, baby."

He slammed a third finger inside, and I gasped while I adjusted to his thick fingers opening me up. "So sexy. I want to press your face against my desk and fuck you on it."

"Do it," I dared.

Images of my face pressed against the wood of his desk while he flipped my dress up and plunged his big cock inside me shot through my horny brain. He'd slap my ass and fist my hair while he fucked me raw, like the animal inside him. The animal he kept locked away until it was time for us to play. Everyone thought Declan MacGregor was so mild-mannered, but they didn't know the alpha I knew in the bedroom.

"You have to be quiet, love," he whispered.

I nodded. "I'll be quiet, I swear."

He gripped my jaw in his hands. "You know what will happen if you don't." He slapped my ass to demonstrate, but that made me want to misbehave even more. He spread my legs wider and curled his fingers up, finding that spot that set me off. "Come on my hand first."

I nodded and rocked my hips, pressing his thick fingers deep inside me. I felt his raging dick against my leg while I fucked myself on his hand. His fingers pumped in and out of me faster and more erratically, and I had to bite my lip to keep myself from screaming out his name.

"Be real quiet as you come all over my hand," he whispered in my ear. "Then you can come all over my big dick."

I nodded and wrapped my arms around his neck, holding onto him while I thrust my hips against his hand. The sound of the music from the party was drowned out by the wet, slick sounds of his fingers moving inside my pussy. He increased the pressure, and I shoved my face into his neck to silence my cries as my orgasm built. I kissed his neck and rolled my hips as he took me over the edge, and I came so hard I thought I saw stars behind my eyes.

He cupped my face and kissed me slowly as I came back down. "Such a good girl."

I nodded. "I'm your good girl."

"Yeah, you are. Undo my belt, love."

I cocked my head at him.

"I changed my mind. I want you to ride me. Undo my jeans and take my cock out."

I did as he asked while he licked my cum off his fingers.

I was so turned on when he moaned at my taste that I lifted up on my knees and slid down on his cock. Declan always filled me like no other man, like we were made for each other, but feeling him bare inside me sent a thrill through me. I'd never let anyone inside me without a condom. We only did it one other time before, and he said we weren't doing that again, but he didn't seem to mind right now.

He slapped my ass while I slid all the way down on his cock, inch by glorious inch. I put my hands on his shoulders and rolled my hips up and then back down.

He slapped my ass hard this time. "Naughty girl."

"What?"

"We need a condom."

I didn't stop my gentle pace as I rode his unsheathed cock, and it didn't seem like he wanted me to.

He tipped back his head. "Fuck, you feel so good. My love, this is a dangerous game."

"Come inside me," I begged. I pressed on his shoulders harder to get better leverage as I rode him faster, feeling another orgasm about to crest above me.

"Lila," he hissed.

"I told you I'm on the pill. Don't you love the feeling of being bare inside me?"

"Fuck yes, it feels amazing, but I always wrap it up."

"Not always."

"Fuck, you're the only woman I've been bare with. Only woman I should've ever been with."

I pretended not to hear that statement, riding him faster instead. His hips lifted off the chair, and he met me with every rise and fall of my strokes. He wrapped my hair around his fist as we moved together in his office chair. He swiped his thumb across my clit, and I slammed back down on his cock until he was buried to the hilt again.

"Come for me, my love. Ride my huge cock like the naughty little witch you are," he growled.

I bit my lip and did as he asked. My thighs were on fire as I frantically rode his cock. He grabbed my throat and pulled me down for a passionate kiss. We kissed through our shared orgasms, moaning into each other's mouths and clinging to each other as the waves of pleasure washed over us.

I broke off the kiss to catch my breath and held his face in my hand. His brown eyes looked at me like I had put a spell on him, like I enchanted him. I kissed him one last time before getting off his lap. I felt his cum dripping down my thighs, and the dirty girl inside wanted to keep it there to remind me of our quickie in his office. But that was gross, so I grabbed a tissue off the desk and slid my hand between my legs to clean myself off.

When I turned back to Declan, he had already zipped up his jeans, but he was running his hands through his hair and looked like I had just rocked his world. It surprised me when he gave me a hard stare.

"What, baby?" I asked sweetly.

"I'm gonna tie you up later and spank that beautiful ass, you naughty little witch."

I grinned. "You loved it."

He pulled me back down into his lap again and pushed my hair behind my ear. "Fuck yeah I did, but Lila, my love, we can't do that again."

Hmm. He said that last time, and yet, we had unprotected sex again.

"Still on the pill. It's okay if we don't use condoms. You're the only man that's been bare inside me."

"Are you sure?"

I nodded and ran a hand down his chest. "If it makes you nervous, you can pull out and paint me with your cum."

"Fuck," he groaned.

I smiled seductively. "You can come all over my tits."

He gripped my hair and gave me a stern look. "Don't make me spin you around and fuck you against my desk."

I gave him an innocent smile. "Why? Have I been a bad girl?"

His grip on my hair tightened, but I loved it. "So, fucking bad."

I got up from his lap and brushed off my dress, making sure there weren't any cum stains on it. That would have been embarrassing. "Okay, well, now that's settled, quit working and come to the party."

He stood up and retrieved my witch hat from where it fell onto the floor. He placed the hat back on my head and spun me around to get the full view of my slinky black dress. He looked at me like he was reconsidering slamming me against his desk and taking me on it.

"Later, baby," I warned him. "Come join me at the party. You know I love Halloween."

He cupped my face. "I know you do, but you're gonna get it so good later."

"Promises, promises!" I teased.

"So bad..." he whispered.

"Party first. Playtime later!" I exclaimed.

A soft smile curled up on his lips, and he let me take his hand and drag him away from his work.

CHAPTER TWENTY

DECLAN

I watched Lila laugh with Gemma, and my eyes roamed across her body, taking in her sexy witch costume. When she came into the office and fucked me in my chair, it had been a welcomed surprise. Now, I was having a hard time telling my dick to wait until later.

I'd admit, I loved all the sexy outfits that Halloween brought out, but especially how she looked tonight. In that black dress, dark makeup, and fuck me heels, she was my dream girl. Would be my dream girl. Always and forever.

"Aw!" Lila cried, and the sound pulled me away from my horny thoughts. I raised an eyebrow, but then I saw my brother and his wife enter the brewery with my niece in Avery's arms.

Nolan was dressed in black jeans and a black button-down, but he had a red cape over his big shoulders and wore red horns on his head. The scowl on his face put the whole devil ensemble together. Next to him, Avery wore a white dress with a halo on her head that Norah kept trying to knock off. Norah was dressed in a little skeleton onesie.

"You guys look amazing!" Gemma cried.

"Aw, look, she matches her uncle!" Lila said and put a hand to her heart.

I smirked. Gemma had given me shit about my boring costume, but I thought it was good enough. I had been too busy being caught up with Lila this past week to think about what to wear. I had a feeling the same was with Lila, since I was pretty sure that dress was just a regular sexy black dress, but the witch hat and her makeup pulled it all together.

Avery unclenched her newborn's hand from around her head. "This is why I didn't put the wings on. Such a little stinker!"

Nolan smiled and took Norah out of her arms. "But she's so cute! Right, Peanut?" Norah grabbed onto my brother's beard in response.

"Norah!" Avery chastised and then shook her head.

"Hey, Avs, you look great," Lila told her.

Avery smiled, and she took us all in. "You all look great, except for Dec. That's such a cop-out costume!"

"I told him that!" Gemma exclaimed, vindicated.

I shrugged. "The place looks great, Gem."

"It's amazing!" Lila agreed.

Gemma's smile got big. "Great! I wanted it to be awesome. We're going to do a costume contest too. It's gonna be so fun!"

I smiled. Gemma got excited about these events, which was exactly why I wanted her in her current position. She was good at what she did.

Lila took a sip of her beer, then she looked at Nolan. "How's the beer coming along?"

"Great! I haven't made a red in a really long time. Your dad's gonna love it."

"He laughed his ass off at the name," she said.

Nolan barked out a big, booming laugh. "I knew he would."

"Only good beer name you've had in a while," Gemma teased.

Nolan glared at her, but it was replaced by a smile when Norah grabbed his beard again. My brother was so soft and squishy for his baby. And Avery. It was cute how they made the grumpy bear of a man change his demeanor. I loved that for my brother. Before Avery got pregnant, he was wound so tight that I had been worried about him.

"How long are you in town for, Lila?" Avery asked.

That was a question that was constantly on my mind. How long was she in town for? She kept saying after Halloween but didn't say she had bought a ticket home yet. So did that mean she'd leave the next day? Any time I asked for clarification, she changed the subject.

Lila shrugged. "I haven't decided yet. My niece asked me to take her trick or treating, so sometime after that."

"I'll go with you," I offered.

"You will?"

I nodded. "We gotta show them all the good spots."

She smiled. "Dec, that would be great."

After a little while, Norah started getting fussy, so Avery and Nolan went home. Gemma was fluttering around the brewery, organizing the costume contest she was holding upstairs in the loft. I peered up there and saw a bunch of costumed patrons waiting in a line. I was glad we were finally making use of that space.

Gemma had transformed the brewery into a spooky spectacle, and I had to admit it looked amazing. Bats were hanging from the ceiling and cobwebs above the bar. There were skulls on the tables, but in the corner, she had moved out some tables for a dance floor. A few people were dancing to the Monster Mash.

I held out my hand to Lila.

She gave me a puzzled look.

"Want to do the Mash?" I asked.

Her face lit up with a huge smile, and she took my hand in hers and dragged me over to the dance floor. We danced a little while, laughing and enjoying each other's company. I felt the weight of all the worrying fall off of me, if only for a moment. This moment, watching her smile as we celebrated her favorite holiday, would be etched in my mind forever. She might leave me in a couple of days, but tonight, I'd make it worth her while.

She wrapped her arms around me. "This is perfect. I love Halloween."

"I know, witchy girl."

She tipped back her head and moved to the beat of the music with me. "It's the best time of the year! Especially here in Drakesville."

"Yeah?"

She nodded, and her witch hat almost fell off her head, but she grabbed it just in time. "Yeah, it's the way the air smells and how pretty the leaves look as they change colors. It's so perfect. And..."

"And what?"

Her hazel eyes gleamed underneath the dim lights. "You're here."

"Yeah?"

She nodded.

I felt like she was trying to tell me something, but I didn't know what. My heart was pounding loud in my chest every time I looked at her. Having her in my arms right now, I didn't want to let her go. But I didn't want to hold her back because her life wasn't here. I kept telling my heart that. Kept telling it she couldn't be ours.

Instead of asking her what she meant, I dipped my head down and took her mouth. She pressed her hand against my chest while she let me devour her. I angled her head to deepen the kiss. Kissing her like this was the last time we would ever be connected. I had a couple more days until she was gone, but tonight felt like a goodbye.

She gave me a heated look when she pulled away. "Can we get out of here?"

"I thought you'd never ask."

I was glad my apartment was literally two doors down. We were gone in a flash, and as soon as we got inside, she was in my arms. Her arms and legs were wrapped around me tightly, and we were all roaming hands and messy kisses as I walked us back into my bedroom.

I deposited her on the bed, and her witch hat went flying. I didn't give two fucks about the mess when I was about to have her again. She stood up and slid the zipper slowly down her dress, then the material fell in a puddle at her feet. I groaned, noticing for the first time that she hadn't been wearing a bra either. Lila stood in front of me naked, save for a pair of sexy stiletto heels.

I tore my shirt off but stopped as she knelt in front of me and undid my jeans. She slid my jeans and boxer briefs down my legs, giving me a naughty grin when she licked the pre-cum off my cock, then pulled it into her mouth.

I gripped her hair in my fist and bucked my hips, fucking her face as she took me down her throat. "Take it," I growled.

She nodded on my dick.

I closed my eyes as the pleasure coursed through my body. I gripped Lila's hair harder, and she took me further inside, licking and sucking her way towards my oncoming orgasm.

I loosened my grip on her hair and pulled my dick out of her mouth.

"What's wrong?" she asked.

I bent to undo the strap on her shoe and lifted her foot out of it. I repeated the action with the other foot. "On the bed, love. Hands above your head."

She obeyed, and I opened the bedside table to grab the wrist restraints. Once I tied her to the bed, I took my time kissing my way up her body.

"Please, Declan," she begged, rocking against her restraints.

"Be good, or I'll tie your ankles up too."

"Please? I need you so bad."

I slid my finger down her slit, finding her already wet. I pressed a thumb against her clit, and she bucked her hips up at me. "You want my cock, love?"

She nodded. "Need it. Now."

I played with her clit a little longer while she whimpered and came all over my fingers.

"Please?" she begged again.

"Okay…" I conceded and went to grab a condom, but she squeezed my waist with her legs. I should have tied up her ankles, too. Such a naughty little witch.

"No condom. I want to feel all of you."

"You sure?" I asked.

Don't get me wrong, her fucking me in my office chair with nothing between us felt amazing, but I was still nervous about going without.

She nodded.

I opened up the drawer and slicked lube down my cock. When I pressed my unsheathed cock inside her, I groaned at the sensation of all of her wrapped around me.

"Fuck, you feel so good," I moaned out.

She wrapped her legs around me, and I moved inside her slowly, not wanting this to ever end. My emotions were all over the place as we moved together with nothing between us. The intimacy of our lovemaking was on another plane. I felt like she was mine, and I was hers, but I knew tonight was more of a goodbye than anything else.

We made slow love, kissing in time with the movement of our bodies together. She rocked against her restraints, but we both loved the fight of it. Of her fighting to touch me when we both knew she couldn't. I cupped her face and kissed her deeply, trying to tell her with my lips all the things I knew I couldn't say out loud.

"Dec," she panted when I slid out and then back in painfully slowly.

I pressed a thumb against her clit and stroked in time with my movements. "Come for me, my love."

She nodded and squeezed her legs around my waist harder. Her hands clenched into fists above her head, and she rode out her orgasm, panting and moaning my name as she came undone beneath me.

"So good," I moaned and increased my pace.

Being bare inside her was dangerous, but I didn't want to stop. She felt too good. I wanted to bust inside her, to make her mine. To brand her with my seed. I was so close to exploding inside her, but I wanted it to last.

"Come inside me. I want it," she begged.

And then I was sliding inside her as hard and fast as I could, pinning her down as I took her with reckless abandon. I was like a rutting beast, and by the way she cried out my name again, she loved every second of it.

"Fuckkkk," I groaned as ropes of cum spilled out of me and inside her as wave after wave of pleasure expelled from my body. I meant to pull out and smear it across her beautiful tits, but she felt too good that I couldn't stop myself.

I grabbed her face and kissed her with all the passion I could muster. I kissed her until I felt myself get soft inside her, then I finally got off of her.

I grabbed a tissue from the bedside table to clean myself up. My sheets were a mess, and that should have made me twitchy. But right now, I didn't care one bit. I undid the restraints above Lila's head and kissed her wrists like I always did after I bound her.

She giggled. "I love that you do that."

I rubbed her wrists. "It's my aftercare. I need it too. Let me grab you a washcloth."

I ran to my bathroom and got her a warm washcloth. I brought it back to her, and she cleaned herself off. "Ew. There's cum on the bed."

I laughed. "Get up. I gotta throw this in the wash."

I was lucky I had a washer and dryer in this unit. It made up for the small space. Lila went to the bathroom while I threw the sheets in the wash and put a clean set on the bed. She jumped into the clean sheets and rolled around in my bed excitedly.

I laughed.

"Best Halloween party ever!" she exclaimed.

I climbed into bed with her and cuddled her. "I wholeheartedly agree."

When I stared at this raven-haired beauty in my bed, when I looked at the smile I put on her face, I wanted to tell her I loved her. I wanted to beg her to stay this time. But I told her all those things long ago, and she hadn't stayed then. I had to be content that this was it. That, in a couple of days, she would leave me again with a shattered heart.

Tonight. I'd enjoy the comfort of her in my arms. I'd think about the hurt much later.

CHAPTER TWENTY-ONE

LILA

I woke to the smell of bacon, and I reached a hand out to find Declan wasn't in bed beside me. I opened my eyes slowly and saw his side of the bed was completely empty. I strained my ears and heard him cooking in his kitchen. The smell of breakfast and strong coffee wafted in from behind the closed bedroom door, and I couldn't help the smile that etched across my face.

The party last night was awesome, and last night in bed with him was amazing. But also bittersweet. When he made love to me, he was saying goodbye. Like he already knew I was going to break his heart. Afterward, when he held me tight, he broadcasted all those feelings. He got quiet, yet needy in the way he held me so close, afraid I'd float away if he let go.

I almost told him I loved him at the brewery. When we were dancing underneath the dim Halloween lights, and he looked at me with his eyes aglow with happiness, I almost let it slip. I couldn't tell him now. Not when I still hadn't decided if I was sticking around.

I needed to make a choice soon. If I wasn't going to move back, telling Declan I loved him, even if it was the truth, would only hurt him in the end. I had already hurt him so much; I couldn't bear to do it all over again.

I checked the time on my phone and frowned when I saw a text from Chad.

CHAD: *My stuff's out of your house. Can you let me know you're okay? Your neighbor said you asked her to get your mail, and you've been gone for over a month.*

Shit. I forgot about that. I should have had the post office hold it for me.

I shot off a quick text to Chad. I didn't want to, but if I didn't, he would pester me.

ME: *Fine. Went home to Pennsylvania to figure some things out.*

I put my phone down and got out of bed. I grabbed one of Declan's t-shirts from his dresser drawer and threw it on.

I opened the door to his bedroom and tip-toed into the kitchen. Declan was humming to the music he was playing and flipping pancakes on the griddle. A plate of pancakes was next to him, and bacon was waiting for us on the table. He cut up some fruit while he waited for the next pancake to cook.

I crept up behind him and wrapped my arms around his waist. He turned in my sneaky embrace and gave me a quick kiss. "There she is!"

"You're making breakfast?"

He nodded. "Coffee's on. It's just about ready."

I went over to the coffeepot and poured some into a mug he had waiting for me. I sipped on it while he finished breakfast. "Is this Wawa coffee?"

"You know it!"

"Mom sends me their ground coffee, but it's not the same as when you go to the store."

"Truth! But still good."

He turned off the burner and brought the stack of pancakes over to the table. I took the seat next to him. We piled our plates up with food, and I moaned at the taste of the deliciously fluffy pancakes in my mouth.

Declan smirked as he ate his own food.

"Thanks for breakfast. You didn't have to."

His hand squeezed my thigh. "I wanted to. What's your plan for today?"

"Dunno. I have some business stuff to do. You'll be at the brewery today?"

He nodded. "Yeah. I figured I'll go in after we're through, and then I have Sunday dinner at Nolan's."

"Oh, right."

"Do you want to come?"

I shook my head. "No. I think I need to be at my own family's tonight. But I'll see you tomorrow to take the kids trick or treating, right?"

"Oh, right. That should be fun. So, when are you going home?"

"Not sure yet. But I'll tell you when I do, okay?"

He nodded, but he seemed unsure. We ate the rest of breakfast in silence, and I couldn't help but feel a thick fog of tension surrounding us. I didn't know when I wanted to go home because I wasn't sure if I even wanted to anymore.

I offered to clean up after breakfast, but Declan said I'd do it wrong. I rolled my eyes. He was such an anal neat-freak. After he was done, we both got dressed and walked out of his apartment together. Before we walked off in different directions, he pulled me flush against his chest and kissed me goodbye.

I melted into the kiss. All my synapses fired off at once when his lips were on mine. I had dated a lot of men since Declan and I broke up. I'd been engaged twice. But none of those men held a candle to him. Kissing those men was like kissing a dead fish. When Declan kissed me, sparks flew, and my body curled against his, wanting more. Kissing him made me feel safe and warm. Like this man was the home I needed to come back to.

When he pulled away, he brushed my hair behind my ear. "I'll see you later, okay?"

I nodded. I felt a pang in my heart when I watched him walk in the other direction. That felt like a kiss goodbye, and I didn't want it to be goodbye. I also didn't understand why he made me feel like it was a goodbye when I was going to see him tomorrow. I hadn't even bought a plane ticket yet. I probably wouldn't leave for another couple of days. We still had a little more time together. So why did it feel like everything was falling apart?

I walked over to the bar and tried to will myself to stop thinking about the weirdness of my love life. The bar had just opened, but Sundays had been busier since I suggested adding Sunday brunch. I found my dad in the office, crunching numbers.

"Hey, Dad," I said as I pulled up a chair beside him.

"Hey, honey. How was the Halloween party?"

"It was good. How do you think things have been going since we did the rebrand?"

"Good," he said, giving me a proud smile. "I have to hand it to you. You did a real good job trying to turn it around."

"Okay..." I trailed off.

I bit my nails and tried to think about how to ask him this question. I wanted the bar to succeed, and I wanted it to stay in the family, but I was afraid my dad would decide not to sell it to me.

"Spit it out, Lila."

"I want to buy the bar."

"What?"

"Brian and Kelsey can't afford to buy it from you, but I can. So I want to buy the bar from you and keep it in the family."

Dad rubbed a hand across his scruffy jaw and stared at me.

Time stood still as he stared at me, and I tapped my foot, waiting for him to give me an answer.

"I want it to go to someone who'll be involved. Not someone who will go back to their life across the country and forget about it."

I gulped. He wasn't going to sell it to me. My dad wouldn't sell to me because I didn't live here.

"What if I moved back?" I blurted out.

What was I doing? Moving back to Drakesville? Did I really want that? Or did I only think I did because I wanted the bar to stay in the family?

Dad raised an eyebrow at me. "Is that what you want?"

I shrugged.

He held up a hand before I said something else. "I want the bar to stay in the family too, but I also want it with someone who's going to be around. Someone who cares about this town and its people. It's not just a bar, it's a community gathering, and that's what it's always been."

I swallowed the lump in my throat. I had a lot of things to think about. And I was running out of time. If I moved back, I didn't have to let Declan go. I didn't have to feel this ache in my chest. Because if I stayed, we could be together again.

"Think about it, honey. It's not a decision you should take lightly."

It certainly was not. I needed more time to consider if that was really what I wanted. If this town and the bar were what I wanted most out of my life. If Declan was what I wanted. I probably knew the answer when I kissed him again for the first time in sixteen years. But I needed to think about it before completely upending my life.

CHAPTER TWENTY-TWO

DECLAN

A smile spread across my face when I walked up to the Sullivans' house and saw Lila standing at the front door waiting for me with Callie on her hip and Cora holding her hand. I adjusted the cape around my neck. I took a long time getting the vampire makeup right, but Lila didn't seem mad that I was late. No, the sexy little witch and her two tiny witches looked giddy to see me.

"Uncle Declan!" Cora cheered and ran to me.

"Cora! What did we say about calling Declan your uncle?" Lila chastised.

"That he's not," she said. "Yet." She muttered that last part under her breath and gave me a wink.

I picked her up and swung her around. "Who's a little witch?" I teased her.

"Me!" she cheered.

Lila laughed. "Okay, my little witches, let's go get your treats. Declan's going to be our vampire escort tonight."

I put Cora down and held out my hand to her. She took

it and excitedly swung her pumpkin candy bucket in her other hand.

Lila let Callie down and took her hand. "Thanks for coming with me. I didn't realize how hard it is to corral two kids."

"No problem. I figured you could use the help. They both look too stinking cute."

Lila beamed. "Thank you. They couldn't decide, and Callie almost had a meltdown, but luckily I found witch hats for us all. So yay, Auntie Lila!"

"Such a good aunt," I teased.

She rolled her eyes as we came up to the first house. I rang the bell and our neighbors, the Adams, fawned over the girls.

"Oh my, a visit by some witches!" Mrs. Adams fake gasped. She winked at me and Lila while she dropped fun-sized candy bars in the girls' buckets.

"What do you say, girls?" Lila reminded them of their manners.

"Thank you!" they cheered. Or at least Callie tried. She was so little she still spoke in baby talk.

We went to a couple more houses, the girls getting more excited about the candy. Lila told them they had to wait until they got home so she could cast protection spells on everything.

I smiled to myself as I listened to her talk and interact with her nieces. Lila would be a great mom one day, and she was an awesome aunt for taking these two out tonight so Brian and Kelsey didn't have to.

"How's Kels doing?" I asked.

"Tired, but she seems okay," Lila said.

"Baby number three, huh?"

Lila laughed. "Well, Brian has four brothers."

"Four?" I exclaimed. "There's a fourth one?"

I knew about Killian since he was in our grade, and Ronan was a grade or two below us, so we knew each other growing up. I hadn't met Finn until the grand re-opening party at the pub. He had the red Murphy hair like Brian, so I probably would have guessed he was one of their brothers had they not told me. I didn't know there was yet another brother.

"Oh, that's because Lachlan's the baby. He's Gemma's age," she explained. "And he lives in Fishtown."

That would explain it. If he lived in the city, I probably didn't know him that well.

I rarely went into the city. Drakesville wasn't in the country or anything. It was a small town close to Philly in a highly populated area. I preferred suburban life over the city. Or maybe I was complacent about living in the same place my whole life.

"He did the photography for the new website."

"Oh. Those were pretty good."

Lila nodded, and we continued to talk as we walked down the street until we made it to my brother's house.

Lila bent down and put her hands on both girls' shoulders. "Okay, my little witches, this is the house Declan grew up in. His big brother lives here with his wife and their baby. So we're gonna knock quietly in case the baby's sleeping, okay?"

Both girls nodded their little heads.

"Baby?" Callie asked and pointed to Lila's stomach.

Lila laughed. "No, sweet pea. No baby for me, but Declan's got a little niece like you were once."

We walked the girls up to the porch, but I had already texted Avery that we were two houses down, so she opened the door before we had time to knock. And Norah was on her hip, wearing the cutest pumpkin costume ever. My niece was so cute.

"Aw!" Lila cried. "She looks so cute!"

"Look at you!" Avery exclaimed as she looked at the little girls. "I'm graced by double witches tonight!"

"Three," I said as I took Norah out of her arms. I rocked Norah, and when I looked at Lila, she had a funny look in her eye when she saw me with my niece.

Avery laughed. "Oh, I didn't even see you there, Lila. You all look great. Wow, Dec, you even dressed up."

"It's Halloween. It's the rules!" Lila exclaimed.

Avery laughed. She wasn't wearing a costume, unless a tired working mom was one, but she had Norah dressed up, so I thought that counted for something. Avery dropped two candy bars in the girls' buckets, then I handed the baby back to her. Norah started to cry immediately.

Avery frowned. "Gee, thanks, Dec."

"Sorry!"

She fixed me with a glare. "One day you're going to have a crying baby of your own, and you'll know my pain."

"One day!" I said.

"Say thank you to Mrs. MacGregor, girls," Lila urged them.

They said their thanks, and we waved to Avery. She waved Norah's little hand for her as we walked to the next house.

"Norah's so cute," Lila said.

I smiled. "Yeah, she is."

"I like Avery."

"Yeah? Me too. She brings the best out in Nol."

Lila squinted at me. "Can I admit something terrible?"

"What's that?"

TEMPORARILY IN LOVE

"Kath sucked, and she and Nol were never right for each other."

Her honesty stunned me, but she was one hundred percent correct. My brother's first wife was the worst. They got married right out of high school, and I think they only did so because Nol needed help raising me. I'd always feel guilty about the burden on my brother after our parents died. Nol didn't resent me for it, but it wasn't easy for him at eighteen being my guardian.

"You're not wrong."

Lila grinned at me, but then her nieces tugged her along, and I had to jog to keep up with them. Those two tiny girls were certainly making us work for it.

We went to a couple more houses until Callie got cranky and Cora had filled up her bucket until it was brimming with candy. In our day, we took pillow cases out and hit up the whole town. But Lila's nieces might be a bit too young for that.

I picked up Callie, and she fell asleep on my shoulder while Lila held Cora's hand as we walked back to her parents' house.

Once inside, Lila took Callie from me and brought her up to one of the guest rooms, where the girls slept. Downstairs in the living room, I inspected the candy for the girls like our parents always did for us.

"Declan? Why can't I call you uncle?" Cora asked.

I blew out a breath. Oh boy, there was a lot to unpack there. I would have loved for her to call me her uncle, but I got why that would be confusing.

"Because, sweetheart, your aunt and I aren't married."

"But why?"

"Your Aunt Lila and I just came back into each other's lives. We're not together like your mommy and daddy."

"Why?"

I sighed. 'Why' seemed to be her favorite question. I didn't know how to answer this tiny interrogator. Why wasn't I married to her aunt? Because she broke up with me a long time ago and avoided me whenever she came back into town. Because I never got the chance to ask.

"Cora," Lila said in a warning tone. "Stop harassing Declan. He was so nice to come trick or treating with us. Say thank you."

"Thank you," she said. "Uncle Declan!"

I smirked at her. This kid sure was going to be a handful.

Lila rolled her eyes and shrugged.

"Okay, kiddo, you can have two pieces of candy tonight," Lila told her.

I nodded to the candy spread out before us. "I inspected both buckets. We're all good."

"Thanks," she said with a sigh. "Did you eat? I was so busy today, I forgot to eat dinner."

"I could eat," I said.

"My mom said there's leftover pizza."

"Works for me."

Lila took the buckets of candy into the kitchen with her while Cora and I went into the living room. We popped on a Halloween cartoon special and sat together. She snuggled into me, and something reached out and pulled at my heartstrings. She might be a little interrogator, but she was a cute kid.

Lila walked back into the living room and handed me a plate of pizza. She sat on the other side of us. Cora had fallen asleep nestled into my side, and I tried not to spill pizza on the top of her head. Man, being a parent seemed exhausting.

"I think she stole my man," Lila joked. "Oh jeez, this special does not hold up!"

"It's a classic!" I argued.

"It looks so old!" she said with a laugh.

I laughed too because she was right.

She looked like she was going to say something else, but then the front door opened, and Brian and Kelsey walked in. Kelsey walked into the living room. She put a hand to her heart when she saw her daughter curled up next to me. Her eyes got all shiny.

Brian groaned. "Baby, no more tears tonight, okay?"

"It's the hormones," she hissed at him. "But look at them, so cute! Where's Callie?"

Lila pointed upstairs. "I put her up in their room."

Brian picked up Cora and held her in his arms. "Thanks for taking them tonight. I owe you."

Lila waved him away with her hand. "It was fun, I don't mind. I had Dec to help corral them, but they were both good."

Kelsey hugged her sister. "We appreciate it so much. It gave us time to have a little date night together."

Brian and Kelsey left not long after that with their sleepy girls in tow.

Lila yawned after we finished watching the Halloween special.

"I should go. You seem tired," I said, giving her thigh a little squeeze.

"You could stay. If you want?"

"Would your parents get weird about that?"

She shook her head. "Nah. Plus, we're over thirty."

I laughed. "Do you want me to stay over?"

She nodded. "I want to be wrapped up in your arms.

Tonight has been perfect. I want to go to sleep knowing you're there."

I nodded. "Okay, love. Let's go to bed then."

She seemed melancholy tonight, and I wondered if she was getting sad about our time ending. She still hadn't said when she was leaving, which was why I came out with her tonight. Although I had to admit, it was fun taking her nieces trick or treating. It made me nostalgic for my childhood. And for all the years we missed hanging out because we avoided each other after our breakup. I had missed my best friend so badly. I wasn't sure how I was going to handle it when she left me again.

I followed Lila up to her childhood bedroom. I took off my cape, and she led me into the bathroom. She rubbed some sort of wipe across my face.

"OW!" I exclaimed.

She gave me a sympathetic smile. "Sorry, baby, this Halloween makeup seems like a bitch to get off. These make-up remover wipes should do the trick, though." She rubbed my face until it felt raw, and then she gave me a kiss. "You'll all good now. Next time, let me do it."

Neither of us questioned that 'next time' because we both knew there would never be a 'next time.' After she washed off her makeup and we brushed our teeth, we crawled into bed together.

"Seriously, will your dad come at me with a bat if he finds us asleep in here?" I asked.

She cackled. "No! My dad was never like that. He trusted I made whatever decisions were right for me. Plus, he loves you."

I pulled her closer against my chest and kissed her neck. "Happy Halloween, my love."

She turned in my embrace. "I'm so glad I got to spend it with you and the girls. All my favorite people."

She gave me a quick kiss, then she promptly fell asleep.

I lay awake staring at the ceiling, wondering when the shit would hit the fan. Wondering how hard it was going to hit me when she walked out of my life again.

CHAPTER TWENTY-THREE

LILA

"Lila," Declan's deep voice boomed in my ear.

I jerked awake and was surprised to find Declan sitting on my bed in his Halloween costume. Then I remembered I had asked him to stay at my parents' house last night. I was addicted to being in his arms and the idea of him leaving last night made me sad.

"Hmm?" I asked and stretched my arms above my head.

He gestured to his outfit. "I gotta go home and do the walk of shame."

A giggle bubbled up from inside my chest. "Sorry. I love sleeping beside you."

He pressed a kiss to my forehead. "I know, my love. I'll see you later, okay?"

I nodded, but then he kissed me goodbye, and I felt like I was going to melt into the bed in a pool of swoon. When he kissed me, it was like I was floating on cloud nine. I didn't realize until I came back to town and started this thing with him how alive his kisses made me feel. How all those other men never made me feel what he did.

He pulled away and pushed a strand of hair out of my face. "I gotta go, love," he whispered.

I squinted at the clock. It was only ten, and I knew the brewery didn't open until noon.

"I have a sales meeting this morning before we open that I forgot about," he explained.

I nodded. "Oh, okay. Thanks for staying last night."

The corners of his mouth tipped up in a smile, and he gave me one last quick kiss goodbye.

I laid back on the bed and watched him go, laughing to myself that he had to leave wearing his vampire costume.

Last night, I had been giddy when I saw Declan actually dressed up for the occasion. In high school, he let me pick our costumes. I hadn't asked him to dress up, so that had been a pleasant surprise. I hadn't planned on going as a witch again, but when Kels and Bri dropped off the girls, they were too excited to pick. When I put the witch hat on, Cora got excited about us being a trio of witches.

I rolled out of bed and got dressed before heading downstairs. I wondered if my parents would say anything about Declan staying over last night. My mom was cheering for us to be back together, so I didn't think so. Plus, we were thirty-four, and my parents didn't lean into the repressed Irish-American thing.

When I walked into the kitchen downstairs, my parents smiled at me over their coffee. "Morning, sweetheart," Mom said.

I grabbed a cup of coffee and sat at the table with them. "Morning."

"How were the girls?" Dad asked.

"Good. It was good to have Declan with me, or they would have been a handful."

Mom raised an eyebrow at me. "Did I just see him leave?"

I nodded.

"Hmm," Dad grunted.

"Did you book your flight home?" Mom asked.

I shook my head.

Nope, still hadn't done that yet. After I talked with my dad about buying the bar, I spoke to my financial advisor about it. He didn't think it was a sound investment if I wanted to make money, but if it was something I wanted to do for my family, he understood why. I still needed to think about all this if Dad was giving me a passive-aggressive ultimatum.

I changed the subject and ate breakfast with my parents. Afterward, I did the dishes and then went upstairs to get dressed. I was planning on going to the bar today to help and see how things were running. If I decided to buy the bar, I'd be a hands-on owner. Brian would still do day-to-day work, but I wanted to be involved in the big picture.

Had I already made my decision? My thoughts told me I had, but I was still uncertain.

My phone vibrated with my alarm to take my birth control. I turned it off and pulled my wallet out of my purse. When I opened my pill pack, something hit me. My period was two days late.

Shit, my period was two days late.

That wasn't normal for me. Sometimes it could be delayed due to stress, but the pill made me regular. Maybe I missed a day, or it came earlier, but never this late.

I took my pill and checked my period tracker app. I should have gotten it already. Sometimes you could miss a period on the birth control I was on, but that hadn't been the case for me. I tried not to think about it. Maybe I'd get it later today.

But I couldn't stop thinking about it.

I went to the bar and waited a couple tables since Siobhan had a doctor's appointment she couldn't miss. She had confided in me that she and her husband were trying to have a baby, and were doing IVF. Then I was thinking about babies again. Maybe Declan was right. We shouldn't have been so careless.

Panic rose up inside me. During a lull in tables, I texted my sister. She was still at work at the high school. School had let out already, but she still had a lot of work to do before her day was over.

ME: *I need to talk to you.*
KELS: *What's up?*
ME: *I'm LATE.*
KELS: [Shocked face emoji]
KELS: *I'm leaving now. Tell Dad I asked for help with something.*

The shift had flipped over, so I quit taking tables and was mostly supervising now. I didn't need to tell Dad I was leaving, but I didn't want him to worry. I hung up my apron and went into the office.

"Hey," I said to him.

"Hey, honey, what's up?"

"I gotta head to Kelsey's for something. Can you cash me out?"

Dad didn't even question what Kelsey needed. He cashed me out, and I left in a rush. Nerves bound up inside me the whole drive to Kelsey's house.

There was no way I was pregnant from this weekend already, but that hadn't been the first time we didn't use a condom. Even though I was on the pill, it wasn't one hundred percent effective. I was old enough to know that, but with my age, I didn't think it was a huge worry. It still might be too early for me to be pregnant. But if I was, I knew it was Declan's, because Chad and I hadn't had sex in months before we broke up.

Kelsey opened the door with her girls clinging to her legs. I laughed, and she gave me a raised eyebrow like, 'this is what you're in for.' The thing was, I wasn't scared about the possibility that I was carrying Declan's baby. No, instead, my brain was picturing us together with one. I envisioned a life together of me staying in Drakesville. A life where I chose Declan.

"In my bathroom, there's a drawer full of them," Kelsey said and nodded to the stairs.

"Thanks," I said and rushed upstairs to her en suite bathroom in her bedroom.

I opened the bottom drawer in the bathroom and found a pregnancy test. I took it out and read the instructions, and did what it said. I capped the end when I was done and sat there waiting. It was agony waiting to find out if the test was going to blink 'Pregnant' or 'Not Pregnant.'

I tapped my foot and sat on the closed lid of the toilet seat. After what felt like an eternity, my phone alarm beeped. I looked at the test, and it blinked back at me with the words 'Not Pregnant.'

I chewed on my lip as I thought. For some reason, I wasn't happy with that result. Which was strange. I should be ecstatic that the result was negative. I didn't want an unplanned pregnancy.

I pressed a hand against my stomach and pictured it growing with a child inside. I imagined Declan's hands on my belly as he assured me everything would be okay. I saw him talking sweetly to my stomach, telling our child how he couldn't wait to meet them. Something squeezed my heart at that future.

I eyed another pregnancy test in the open drawer and pulled it out. I needed to know for sure I wasn't pregnant. I took the other test and felt tears prick my eyes when the second one read 'Not Pregnant' too.

Why was I crying? I should be happy I wasn't pregnant, but disappointment lodged in my chest when I saw the negative results.

It was like all the emotions I'd been shoving down inside were bubbling up to the surface. All the things I didn't want to decide on were demanding answers now. I knew then what I had known for the past few weeks but had been avoiding.

I didn't want to go home to California. I wanted to move back to freaking Drakesville, Pennsylvania. To my nosy hometown and be with the man I loved. Declan was the only man I had ever loved, and it may have taken us several years to get here, but thinking I was pregnant and finding out I wasn't solidified my feelings.

I wanted to be with Declan. I wanted to be with him so badly, and I didn't want to leave him with a broken heart, not again.

When my sister came to find me, I was wiping away my tears and staring down at the negative pregnancy test.

She knelt beside me. "Oh, Lila, it'll be okay."

I shook my head. "No. I'm not pregnant."

She pulled back and gave me a funny look. "Oh. Then what's with the tears?"

"I'm kinda disappointed."

Her brow creased as she stared at me.

I sighed. "I want to have a baby."

"Oh!" she exclaimed. "Did you try to do this on purpose?"

I shook my head. "No. But when I was sitting here, it hit me...I want that with him. I want to get married to him and have lots of cute near-sighted babies."

"And you want to buy the bar?"

I nodded. "Dad passive-aggressively said he'd only sell it to me if I move back."

My sister grabbed my hands. "Oh, Lil, you don't have to buy the bar. If Dad sells, Brian and I will figure it out."

"But...I want to. I've been feeling this pull to stay here. I don't want to be a lawyer anymore. And I definitely don't want to go home with my heart shattered because I let Declan go again."

"I want to make sure you're doing it because you want to."

I nodded. "I'm sad I'm not pregnant. But it made me realize how much time I lost with Declan. I don't regret going to Stanford. It allowed me to have the money to buy the bar, but I regret how it took me sixteen years to come back to him. Years I wasted on awful men. Years without the one man I loved more than anything. So many lost years without my best friend."

Kelsey hugged me. "I knew he was the only one for you, but unlike Mom, I wanted you to figure that out on your own. So what's the plan?"

I sighed. "I gotta go home."

Her face fell. "I'm confused."

I shook my head. "No, I'm coming back, but I gotta go home and sell my house and get my finances in order. And tell Dad I'm moving back."

She held a hand up. "Okay, slow down. You don't need to go home this very second. How about you talk to Dad first, and then you go talk to Declan? Tell him everything you just told me."

I nodded and tossed the pregnancy tests in the trash.

She was right. I didn't need to rush home. Before I did all that, I needed to talk to Declan and tell him how I felt. The whole time I was here, we were holding back because we knew this was going to end, but I didn't want it to end. The moment I kissed him on the zipper, I knew I was never going back. I knew my heart wanted to stay.

I stood up and my sister hugged me. "I'm so glad you're moving back. I just wanted it to be your decision."

I nodded. "This is what I want. I better go talk to Dad."

I hugged her goodbye, got into my rental car, and went to my parents' house. I didn't know if Dad was still at the bar, but when I walked inside, I found him and my mom starting dinner.

"Hey, honey!" Mom said to me.

I walked into the kitchen, and they both had a look of concern on their faces. "I'm moving home," I announced.

"Okay..." Dad trailed off.

Mom clapped her hands and ran over to me, enveloping me in a great big hug. "Oh, honey, that's the best news ever!"

"And I want to buy the bar and take care of it so you can retire," I continued. "And I want to marry Declan MacGregor."

A small smile curled up on my dad's lips. "Okay, honey, but I think you need to tell him that last one, not us."

I took a shaky breath and ran my hand through my hair. "Yeah. And then I need to go home and sell my house."

"What about your law career?" Mom asked.

I shook my head. "I don't regret my success, and I had a great career, but I work eighty hours a week and go home to an empty house with no social life. And my fiancé, who I didn't even like all that much, cheated on me with his damn secretary! And I didn't even care! I want to own the family bar and keep it running. I miss the seasons and want to eat real Philly Cheesesteaks and have people say, 'Go Bulldogs' to me as a greeting. And for people to stop making fun of me for pronouncing it 'wooder,' which is the correct way. And I miss Wawa coffee! I want to have real, good Wawa coffee. And I want the man I love to know that he's the only person I've loved, and I wished it hadn't taken me sixteen fucking years to figure it out!"

I was out of breath after I ranted it all out, but when I looked at my parents, they were holding in their laughter.

"What?" I asked.

Mom's smile could have made the Cheshire Cat jealous. "Oh, honey, go get your man."

I hugged my mom tight. "I was so stupid. I shouldn't have avoided him for all these years."

Mom stroked my hair, and then she pulled back to look at me. She cupped my face. "You're stubborn like your father, but Declan loves you. Now go tell him you love him too. And then get started on making me more grandkids."

I laughed. "Mom!"

She shrugged. "What? You're not getting any younger."

I laughed again, but I hugged her tight. Then I walked over to my dad and hugged him too. "I know you think it's ridiculous for me to throw away my career, but I want the bar, and I want to continue with the family business."

Dad frowned. "It's not that. If you want the bar and you want to take it over, I'll support you. But only if *you* want to do it. That's why I said I'd only sell if you moved back. I didn't think you'd do it, but I wanted you to. I wanted my daughter back even if she's gonna steal my job!"

"It's what I want. I've been unhappy in my career. When Chad cheated on me, it made me reevaluate a lot of things about my life."

Dad pushed me away. "Go on then, go get Declan. We'll see you later."

I spun around and was out of the house in a flash. I needed to tell Declan everything, and I needed to tell him now. Before I got on a plane and changed my mind.

CHAPTER TWENTY-FOUR

DECLAN

"What's up your ass?" my brother growled at me as we went over the numbers.

I ran a hand through my hair and didn't know where to begin. One, Annie hit on me again today, so I made Nolan talk to her about it being inappropriate, which he literally growled at me about making him do that. And two, I was pretty sure Lila was going to leave and not tell me. Probably soon.

"He's cranky because Lila's going home soon!" Gemma answered for me from the other side of the room.

I shot her a glare.

She shrugged. "What? It's the truth."

Nolan rubbed a hand across his beard and gave me an 'I told you so look.'

"I don't want to talk about it," I snapped.

Nolan raised an eyebrow. "I told you to be careful around her."

"How about you get off my dick?" I snarled.

He kept his eyebrow raised and sighed. "Okay, you remember when I wasn't seeing things clearly with Avery, and you told me I was suffering from stupid man syndrome?"

I wanted to laugh. He *had* been suffering stupid man syndrome then. He was so convinced Avery didn't feel the same way, but if anyone looked at either of them, they would have seen how hopelessly in love they were with each other. Nolan hadn't been listening to reason back then. Maybe I should have listened to Nolan when he told me to be careful around Lila. It pissed me off because I knew she was about to leave, and my heart was on the verge of breaking again.

"Dude!" Gemma exclaimed. "Tell her how you feel."

"What?"

"Tell her you love her, dummy," Nolan agreed.

"Maybe it will make her stay," Gemma urged.

"I am staying!" came Lila's voice from the doorway.

I jerked my head up at her entrance. She stood there with a look of determination on her face. Gemma and Nolan shared a confused look, and they quickly darted out of the office to give Lila and me some privacy.

"You what?" I asked, furrowing my brow as I processed her words.

She walked over to me and stood in front of my desk. "I have to go home." She held up her hand before I could get a word in edgewise. "Let me finish. I have to go back to California to sell my house because I'm buying the bar and moving home."

I stared at her unblinking as her words washed over me. She was staying. She was buying her parents' bar and moving here. The gears were turning in my brain because none of this computed to me. She had been so clear that we could only be temporary.

"Declan!" her voice snapped me out of my thoughts.

"Why?" I blurted out.

She frowned and looked taken aback. "Why? Because I took a freaking pregnancy test today."

Shit.

Shit. Shit. Shit.

"Okay, okay, this is fine. We'll be okay," I started rambling. My brain was already calculating the cost to raise a baby and everything we'd need. "We'll need stuff for the baby, and to read the books, but Nolan and Avery will help with that. I'll move out of my apartment, and we can start looking for a house in town. We'll be fine. I know we didn't plan this, but we'll figure it out together."

"Oh my god, will you let me speak?" she asked with an annoyed huff.

"Huh?"

"Dec, I took a pregnancy test, and it was negative. I took a second one to be sure, and then I realized I was upset it was negative. Because from the moment I kissed you on the zipper, I knew I was in trouble, and I was never going back to California."

I stared at her, dumbfounded.

"Please say something, Dec. I'm trying to tell you that you're the only man I've ever loved, and I should've moved back a long time ago. I shouldn't have let you go when I went to Stanford. Maybe we could have survived the long distance, but—"

She jolted when I leaped from my chair and rushed over to her. I didn't let her continue talking. Instead, I pulled her flush against my chest and slanted my mouth on hers. She wrapped her arms around my neck, and I cupped her face as I deepened the kiss. I kissed her like it was the first time, like if I didn't devour her mouth, she would slip away. I kissed her like I was trying to brand her lips with mine.

When we finally came up for air, she smiled up at me. I slid a hand down and rested it against her stomach. "You were really upset you're not pregnant?"

She nodded sheepishly. "I know, it's ridiculous, but while waiting for the results, I was thinking about us having a baby. Picturing us having a family together, of our child growing inside me. And I want that. I know what I want out of my life—you."

I framed her face with my hands. "My love, that's all I've ever wanted since we were fourteen years old."

She laughed. "You did not! We didn't even start dating until we were sixteen."

I kissed the back of her wrist. "Yeah, but I knew then what I wanted most. Nolan makes fun of me for how I've pined for you for so long, but I'm glad no one else was good enough for me. I'm glad I waited for you."

She cringed. "I don't deserve you, Declan MacGregor. Not one bit, but I love you with all of my heart."

"And you want my babies?" I joked.

She grinned. "I do! So much! I want to get married to you, have babies with you, and wake up every day in your arms."

"I want that too. I've always wanted that. But maybe we chill on the marriage talk right this second?"

She shook her head. "No, baby, I'm getting old. I need that MacGregor baby now."

I laughed. "Patience, my love, you know I like to set the pace."

She grinned. "And I love that about you."

My mind was spinning in a thousand directions. Lila, the only woman I ever loved, wanted me. She wanted to marry me and have my babies, and she was moving back to Drakesville.

I pulled back. "You're really going to leave the career you built up over the years behind for me?"

She nodded. "Dec, I don't want to be a lawyer anymore. And working at the bar the past couple of weeks, I want to do that. I'm moving back, and I'm doing something different with my life. That's all."

"Okay, well, let's go find us a flight!"

"What?"

"You said you need to go home and sell your house, right? I bet you have to pack it up too, huh?"

She nodded.

"Well, I'm coming with you. I'll be there with you every step of the way."

Her smile cracked her face, and then she kissed me again.

🍁

"Oh my god, that's it!" Lila exclaimed and taped up the last box.

I grinned as I scrubbed down the counter in her kitchen. Her place in Palo Alto was baller as fuck, but a pain in the ass to clean. We'd been here for about a week trying to pack up all her stuff and see what we could sell. She was going to sell it furnished since trying to move all of it across the country would be too expensive and a headache. I told her we'd get new stuff when we bought a place in Drakesville. My eyes nearly popped out of my head when I saw the asking price when her listing went live. She would definitely have no problem affording to buy her parents' bar.

"Are you sure you want to throw your career away?" I called to her.

She walked into the kitchen and put her hands on her hips. "Baby, we talked about this. I wasn't happy. I'm much happier working at the pub."

I smiled. Since we changed the name, she started calling it the pub instead of the bar. She had already made it her own. She stormed into the place a month and a half ago and made changes left and right like she was in charge, and now she was. She and her dad still needed to work out the bill of sale, but the plan was to sell her house, buy the pub, and then we would live happily ever after.

"I want to make sure this is what you really want," I said.

She walked over to me and put her arms around my neck. "You're what I want, Dec. I want to move back to Drakesville. I miss the seasons and cheesesteaks."

I smirked. "Just those two reasons?"

"And watching the Bulldogs!"

I laughed. "You're ridiculous. You can watch our terrible hockey team from here."

She wrinkled her nose. "It's not the same. Hey! We should go to a game sometime soon. I can't remember the last time I went to a hockey game for a team I actually like."

I laughed. "Yeah, okay, love. Nolan and Avery would love that. They're both such Bulldogs fiends."

"Double date!" she cheered.

I shook my head. "Ridiculous."

"You love me."

"Damn straight, you're mine."

"And I'm yours."

She cupped my face. "Hey, guess what?"

"What's that?"

"I don't have my period anymore. So what do you say, we get a head start on our future?"

"Wait."

I took her right hand in mine and slipped the Claddagh ring off it. She gave me a curious look, but then she got misty-eyed when I slipped it onto her left hand with the crown facing outwards. One day, I'd take her hand and change the direction of the crown. Not today, but soon.

I kissed the back of her palm. I gave her this ring a long time ago. Even then, I knew it was a promise that she'd always be mine.

"One day, I'll get you a better engagement ring, but this is my promise to you," I told her.

She shook her head. "No, Dec. You proposed to me a long time ago. I just didn't realize it. Maybe that's why nothing ever worked with anyone else. It's probably why I avoided you every time I came home."

I gave her a suspicious look. "Yeah, that's a mighty feat in our small town."

"I usually wouldn't leave the house. Drove my family nuts, but that's why I only came home on the holidays. And sometimes not even then. I wish I hadn't been so immature, but I knew if I saw you, I'd be under your spell again. I never would have finished my degree."

"Let's get one thing certain: I'm under your spell. Always have been, always will be."

She rested her forehead against mine and kissed me softly. "I love you so much, Declan Patrick MacGregor. You're the one I've always been waiting for."

"I love you too, Lila Catherine Sullivan. More than you could ever know."

She jumped up into my arms and kissed me like she needed my lips on hers to breathe air. I kissed her back with the same ferociousness and took her upstairs to start our future together.

EPILOGUE

LILA

HALLOWEEN THE NEXT YEAR

I put a hand on my stomach as my sister fixed my veil. Her perfume was making me want to puke, but I didn't have the heart to tell her why. I hadn't even told Declan yet. I thought the nausea had just been nerves about the wedding, but I took a test on a hunch this morning. It definitely wasn't an oops, since Declan and I had been actively trying to get pregnant all year.

Kelsey moved so Lizzie could inspect my makeup. I was glad Kelsey advised me on black bridesmaid dresses versus orange for my Halloween wedding. My bridesmaids looked so classic in their gowns. Avery and Gemma looked at me through the mirror with big smiles on their faces.

Since I moved back to Drakesville, these four women had been in my corner. Especially the Jensen sisters, who were going to become family now that I was marrying Declan. Declan still said Gemma was a PITA, but I knew he loved her like a sister, and so did I.

Lizzie fixed my lipstick. "You look gorgeous. He's gonna freak."

"Thanks," I said and wiped an invisible wrinkle from my dress.

Declan and I weren't dressing in costumes for the occasion. Our wedding might be on Halloween, but it had a more harvest aesthetic than a spooky one. But I wanted my dress to be a little unconventional. It was a gorgeous white ball gown that had a black lace motif on the bodice and again on the hemline. When Gemma found it for me, I nearly cried at how perfect it was.

"You look like a gothic princess!" Gemma exclaimed.

"Dec will love it," Avery agreed.

I nodded.

I was so nervous. Not for the wedding, I was good with that. We were having it at the farm where we picked pumpkins because they also did weddings in their barn. When we were looking for locations, and I found that out, we both knew it was absolutely perfect.

I looked in the mirror and held my stomach. I felt a wave of nausea wash over me.

I groaned before I rushed into the bathroom. Kelsey and Lizzie were behind me in a flash, holding back my hair and making sure I didn't get any vomit on my dress.

Kelsey handed me a travel-size bottle of mouthwash, and I gargled in the sink while she tapped her foot impatiently behind me.

"You okay?" Lizzie asked.

I nodded. "It's...morning sickness."

"I knew your boobs looked bigger!" my sister said with

indignation.

I looked down at my boobs. When we did the fitting, I thought the bodice was a little tighter, but my tailor took it out to fix it. She thought maybe she had gotten the measurements wrong.

"Does Declan know?" Avery asked from the other room.

I brushed my teeth to get the taste of vomit out of my mouth. I had come prepared, but now I needed to fix my lipstick. I wiped my mouth, but Lizzie tilted my face down toward her and fixed it for me.

"You're good. Congrats, mama!" she said and gave my hand a little squeeze.

I smiled. "Dec doesn't know yet. We've been trying since we got back together."

"Aw, he's gonna be so excited!" Gemma cried.

Avery pinned her sister with a look. "You're next."

A look of terror came across Gemma's face. "Hell no! You have enough babies between you all that Felix and I get to be the fun aunt and uncle."

I rolled my eyes. Gemma and Felix were strictly in the 'no kids' club. Good for them, but that was definitely not something I wanted. I was so excited that I was marrying the love of my life, and we were already starting a family together.

Kelsey squeezed my hand. "Congrats, sis. Now, are you ready?"

I nodded. "Yes. I should have been ready to marry Declan a long time ago."

"But he waited for you, so you know he's a good one," Kelsey said and handed me my bouquet of orange, yellow, and red flowers.

A smile broke out across my face. "He's the best man I've ever known."

"And you make him less serious!" Gemma cut in.

I laughed. I loved Gemma. She was a hoot, but she was right. My future husband could be uptight. I could only imagine what he was going to be like while I was pregnant. But I was excited to watch our child grow inside me, to see the life we created together. All my dreams were about to come true, and I couldn't be happier.

My mom came into the room. "You all ready?"

I nodded.

Mom walked over to me and pushed a strand of my dark hair behind my ear. "Oh, Lila, you look gorgeous. It looks like a perfect harvest wedding."

"It's exactly what I wanted."

She ushered us outside. We had been getting ready in the farmhouse, but the wedding was outside underneath the pretty fall leaves. I watched my bridesmaids walk down the aisle with the groomsmen while I waited for my entrance. My dad came up to me and looped his arm through mine.

"You look gorgeous, honey," he told me.

"Thanks, Dad."

I took a breath, and then I was walking down the aisle with my dad. Declan looked misty-eyed when he finally saw me. He was wearing his glasses and was in a nicely tailored black suit. Behind us was a trellis of fall leaves with two huge pumpkins on each side. Everything looked so perfect, and so far, the weather had cooperated.

Declan took my hands as we waited for the pastor to start the service. Despite my Irish-Catholic upbringing, I wasn't that religious, nor was Declan, so we weren't having a traditional wedding. The only tradition we wanted was an Irish wedding blessing read and a handfasting. I already had a Claddagh ring which I kept as my engagement ring, but we also picked out matching wedding bands.

The pastor told everyone to take their seats, and he started the ceremony. "Welcome, everyone. We gathered Lila and Declan here today before their family and friends to make a statement of their commitment to each other. We celebrate the coming together of the families of MacGregor and Sullivan with their love. First, we'll have the mother of the bride read an Irish blessing for the wedding."

My mom stood up and smiled at us through tears as she spoke. "May you always walk in sunshine. May you never want for more. May Irish angels rest their wings right beside your door."

She kissed my cheek and then did the same for Declan.

The pastor turned to Declan. "Do you, Declan, take this woman to be your lawfully wedded wife, in sickness and in health, for as long as you both shall live?"

"I do," Declan said.

The pastor turned to me. "Do you, Lila, take this man to be your lawfully wedded husband, in sickness and in health, for as long as you both shall live?"

I was trying so hard to keep the tears from falling as I looked at the man I loved. "I do."

"Declan and Lila have chosen rings as a symbol of their love."

Declan turned to Nolan, and his brother handed him the ring. Declan took my hand and slid the silver band onto my finger. "Lila, I give you this ring as a symbol of my love. You're my one and only, my best friend, and I promise to love you forever and always."

Kelsey brought over Declan's ring to me, and I repeated the action for him while I looked into his eyes. "Declan, I give you this ring as a symbol of my love. Thank you for waiting for me. You're my best friend and the only man I've ever loved. I promise to love you forever and always."

I stared at the rings on our joined hands and felt my emotions pouring out of me. I half thought that was my pregnancy hormones, but I was so happy I could burst.

The pastor brought out orange and black ribbons and placed them on top of our joined hands. "The couple will celebrate today with a handfasting ritual. I bind these cords now to join the couple as one." He wrapped the ribbons around our hands and tied them together. "Let their bond never be shaken."

He held up our bound wrists to show the crowd. "I now pronounce these two married. Declan, you can kiss your bride!"

The pastor dropped our hands, and Declan slanted his mouth onto mine. Our friends and family were yelling and cheering, but I didn't care when Declan kissed me as my husband for the first time.

I melted into him, and I couldn't stop the tears from falling. We pulled away, and he wiped the tears from my eyes. We walked down the aisle bound together, my heart so full of love.

After the ceremony, it was a whirl of getting pictures taken by Lachlan, who was amazing and made everything so easy. The barn was lit up with twinkling white fairy lights, the tables had jack-o'-lanterns as the centerpieces, and everything looked so amazing. We opted for cupcakes from the bakery in town instead of a cake. We had an assortment of pumpkin spice and apple cider flavors, and they all looked so good, even though I felt like I would throw up if I ate one.

"Hey, you want the pumpkin beer, right?" Declan asked when we finally sat down to eat dinner after the first dances were done. Since my husband owned a brewery, of course, our wedding was flowing with its beer.

I shook my head and rested my hand on my stomach. My sister had gotten me a ginger ale, and I had been sipping that slowly, hoping not to throw up again. I kept pushing my food around on my plate, afraid I couldn't keep anything down.

Declan frowned. "My love, what's wrong?"

I smiled and put his hand on my stomach. "I have to tell you something."

His eyes widened behind his glasses. He took them off and rubbed the bridge of his nose as it all washed over him. He put his glasses back on and searched my face. "Really?" he breathed out, disbelief marring across his face.

I nodded. "I took a test this morning."

"You're really pregnant?" he asked again, putting both of his hands on my stomach.

"I know we've been trying for a while, but...it finally happened," I told him with a shrug.

"So, no beer for you. I love you so much, Lila Sullivan."

I shook my head and wrapped my arms around the back of his neck. Our wedding guests were tapping their forks against their glasses to get us to kiss, as was tradition, but all I cared about was the man in front of me.

"I told you, it's Lila Sullivan-MacGregor now."

Declan grinned. "I thought you didn't want to change it."

I shook my head. "I'm gonna hyphenate it, so our baby can carry on both our names. Maybe one day they can buy the pub from me and take it over."

"I love you so much."

Then he kissed me again, and everyone else melted away as Finn Murphy's band played a low Celtic tune to the sound of my happily ever after.

ACKNOWLEDGMENTS

I'm sad to report that this is the end of the MacGregor series! This series was always meant to only be three books, even when I kept saying it was going to be a one-off. It might not be the last you hear of the town of Drakesville, PA, though, so stay tuned.

I have a lot of people to thank for helping bring this book to you. Firstly my betas - J Lynn, Chris, and Kat. Thanks so much for your guidance on yet another book.

Also to my editors Leah Francic and Kate Seger. Especially Leah for rolling with my unhinged email when I said I wanted to add a fourth book to this year's publishing schedule. I couldn't have done it without you.

I'm so excited this book is out now and you can finally binge the whole series. I love writing in this world, and I hope to expand with some spin-offs in the near future. More to come on that soon, but in the meantime check out my hockey series - The Philadelphia Bulldogs as I will be publishing more in that series in the year to come.

I hope you all love Declan and Lila as much as I do!

ALSO BY DANICA FLYNN

PHILADELPHIA BULLDOGS

Take The Shot

Score Her Heart

Against The Boards

The Chase

MACGREGOR BROTHERS BREWING COMPANY

Accidentally In Love

Trapped In Love

ABOUT THE AUTHOR

Danica Flynn is a marketer by day, and a writer by nights and weekends. AKA she doesn't sleep! She is a rabid hockey fan of both The Philadelphia Flyers and the Metropolitan Riveters. When not writing, she can be found hanging with her partner, playing video games, and reading a ton of books.